# THE BULLS

# THE BULLS

## BOOK TWO

### JOHN STONE

fanny press

Kenmore, WA

**fanny**press

For more information visit www.fannypress.com

All rights reserved. No part of this book may be reproduced or transmitted in any form or by any means, electronic or mechanical, including photocopying, recording, or any information storage and retrieval system, without permission in writing from the publisher.

This is a work of fiction. Names, characters, places, brands, media, and incidents are either the product of the author's imagination or are used fictitiously.

The Bulls
Copyright © 2024 by John Stone

ISBN: 978-1-684921-33-1 (Trade Paper)
ISBN: 978-1-684921-34-8 (eBook)

Library of Congress Control Number: 2023945650

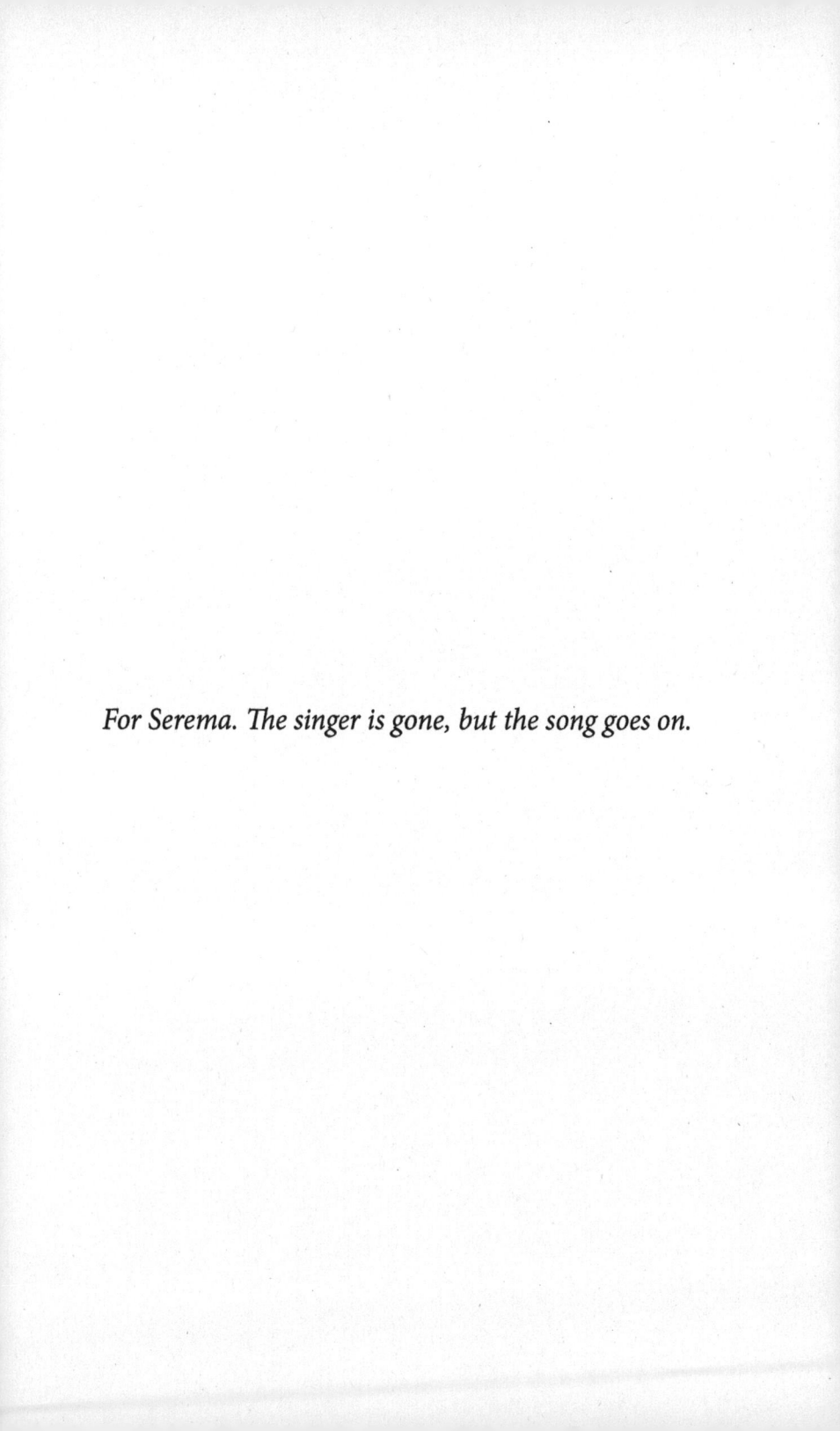

*For Serema. The singer is gone, but the song goes on.*

# 1

"Tell me again," Diane said to me as she more slowly than usual applied her makeup. "why I need to meet this woman?"

"Because Eugene wants us to," I explained for what may have been the tenth time. "And you like fucking Eugene." I was seated in the chair that had been placed in the corner of our bedroom scant weeks before and where I was used to sitting to watch illicit activities, and not talk about them. Bending to tie my shoe I continued." So not meeting her might fuck things up." I giggled as I said the last part, which earned me a derisive look from my wife.

"Hmmph," she grunted in reply. "Just so you know, I am seriously reexamining the policy of letting you socialize with my men." The "my men" was meant to sting me, which it did less than it had at one time. I genuinely liked Eugene, which was a departure from Diane's first Bull, Dan, who considered me only as worthy of abuse, which he was more than happy to provide. Eugene treated me with respect for the most part. There was the undercurrent of him as the superior alpha male, with me as the beta. That was the life of a cuckold. Eugene was subtle about it, and the week after he had come to our home for a dual purpose, to fuck my wife and to help her humiliate her now former bull, he had asked that we meet, just us. We did so at a local place that I wasn't aware we both went to, Costas.' We sat in a booth, out of the mainstream of what was a small crowd (it was Tuesday) so we could talk. Eugene was discreet. He went there often. The last thing he wanted to do was fulfill in the minds of the mostly white patrons their stereotype of him as a "BBC."

He was, however, very big. In ways that showed publicly and those that did not. He was also very black, with skin the color of burnished mahogany. There was no hint that in his lineage any "cream had been added to the coffee." At 6 foot 6 and 280 pounds, I could envision him running down a lion on the Serengeti, even as he sipped his Michelob Ultra seltzer in a suburban bar on a Tuesday as we casually discussed him coming to my house on a regular basis to ravage my wife, whom he would not have to run down.

"So," Diane asked, finally getting her lipstick just so and her eye shadow perfect," tell me again what you and Eugene discussed." As she spoke, she went into her closet and showed me two dresses still on their hangers. I shook my head as she held each up for me to see.

"You are meeting your lover's wife," I reminded her. "Think, friendly, not femme fatale."

She shook her head and made a face. It was the face she always made when she knew I was right and didn't want to admit it. Despite the face, she went back into the closet and came out carrying a pair of jeans and a cute but conservative top. I was going to say something in support of her choices but decided it would be counterproductive, so I merely smiled.

"We talked about how I would handle this whole . . . 'thing.'" I said it tentatively, still not sure how to categorize what we had begun that night at a downtown bar and how our lives had undergone seismic change. "He's concerned about my reaction, unlike someone else we both knew."

Diane's response was simply, "MmmHmm," as she squeezed into the jeans she had chosen. They seductively hugged her pretty, pantied fanny. Maybe too much for the intention of the evening, but I stayed silent. As she slipped the top over her braless breasts, I shook my head.

"What?" She said using the astonished tone she always did when she was pretending to not know what I meant.

"Would you go braless to a job interview?" I asked. She grinned.

"Depends on the interviewer," she replied smugly.

"Well," I responded, "This interviewer is the ostensibly straight wife of the man you want to repeatedly debauch you. My advice would be a bra would be a way to dress for success."

She looked at me sourly and grudgingly pulled off the top, put on a bra, and put the top back on.

"Better," I said in what I hoped was a complimentary manner. The attempted compliment only earned me another, "Hmmph." as she stormed from the room.

"Okay spoilsport," she said testily, "Let's get this over with."

## 2

"**S**O, DO YOU COME HERE OFTEN?"
The question would have sounded like a pickup line had it not come from Eugene's wife Gayle, a very attractive Black woman in her fifties. Since she directed the question to neither one of us in particular, I answered for both of us.

"Occasionally," I explained. "We like Mexican food, and this is our favorite." The place was called "Garcia Seeya" and the food was very good. So were the margaritas, and so we each availed ourselves of one. One of the advantages of my having talked with Eugene earlier in the week was a chance to understand the more mundane preferences of each other and our wives. I had found that Gayle loved Mexican food. Diane preferred Italian, but since she would get her way in most other things going forward, I felt Gayle's tastes should prevail in this instance.

"More drinks folks?" The waitress asked politely, to which my three dinner companions replied yes happily while I declined.

"I'd better not," I said, "I'm driving."

"Gayle and I Ubered over so we wouldn't have to worry," Eugene informed us. As the husband of the woman he was going to have wanton sex with, I was comforted to know he was a responsible person. Typical small talk ensued until the food arrived, at which point conversation slowed. At no point did we speak of what had happened between Eugene and Diane and what would happen again in the very near future. I already knew Gayle had health issues that precluded sexual relations, but she understood his needs. Unlike me, she didn't want to see it. Or have her nose rubbed in it, also unlike me.

Dinner concluded and we went toward the exit. Shaking hands, exchanging hugs, and saying how we needed to do this again and meaning it.

"Excuse me a second," Eugene said looking at his phone. "I forgot I need to call our Uber."

I waved him off. "Don't do that," I told him. "Let me take you home."

They thanked me and got into the Lexus SUV I was driving that year. The home I drove to was not too far from us. Our home was very nice and as much as was needed for Diane and me. Gayle and Eugene's house was mammoth. Tastefully and expensively landscaped with a circle drive in front. I pulled into the entryway and parked.

"Care to come in for a nightcap?" Gayle asked with the warmth and sincerity that had marked the evening. I accepted providing they had club soda. My wife politely demurred saying she had an "early morning." We said our goodnights and drove off. We were quiet for a short while until Diane got a text and finally broke the silence.

"Gayle's out of town next weekend," She declared happily. "So, Eugene is spending it with us."

# 3

FRIDAY NIGHT FINALLY CAME AND SO did my wife. Noisily with Eugene's shaft buried deep inside her hungry cunt. He had arrived around seven and by 7:15 she was dragging him to our bedroom as I cooked and listened to the sounds of passion drifting down the hall to the kitchen. They hadn't closed the door, I assumed on purpose so I could voyeuristically participate and not burn our evening meal. Finally, at about 8 or a few minutes after, my wife's lover strode down the hall asking, "What's for dinner?" Eugene was one hungry Bull, having worked up his appetite on and in my wife.

"Jack," Eugene told me as he finished the last morsel of lasagna, "That was delicious. Thank you so much."

Eugene was obviously a member of the clean plate club, and I removed it and reached for Diane's, which still had some remnants on it. Knowing she was done; I took it and mine and headed to the kitchen.

When I came back to the dining room Diane and Eugene were talking quietly. They stopped once I reappeared, and both looked at me. They smiled. I smiled and finally, my wife spoke.

"Jack," she said, "Eugene thanked you for the lasagna. Isn't there something you want to thank him for?"

As I stood looking at them, my smile was the only one that faded. Not because I didn't know what she meant, but because I did. Finally, Diane nodded expectantly, and I cleared my throat.

"Eugene," I began hesitantly, "Thank you." I stopped the statement there, knowing that Diane would consider it not enough.

She did not, as she prompted me, again, "For . . . ?"

"For . . . fucking my wife." I continued, hoping it was as far as it went. Of course, it was not.

"Because . . ." She said, continuing to urge me on.

"Because I can't do it properly. Because I can't satisfy her. Because I can't meet her needs." I blurted it out. All of it. What I knew to be the truth, and as I said it, I let the shame wash over me like an ocean wave, as it carried me out to sea. In spite of myself, I began to harden as I rode the current.

If I expected my wife to be embarrassed for me, to be distressed at my humiliating admission, I'd have been wrong. She was beaming like a mother whose child just won a spelling bee.

If I had expected Eugene to gloat, I'd have been wrong. His smile was benevolent. Indulgent.

"You are welcome, my friend," he replied generously, as my wife chimed in.

"And later, he plans to do it again," She added happily.

"After dessert," Eugene added his smile broadening. The Hungry Bull seemed determined to satisfy all his appetites. Diane laughed.

"After dessert," she reiterated "Oh, and after dessert, would you like to watch, darling?"

The pair looked at me smiling, awaiting the expected answer as my cock twitched uncontrollably in my pants.

"Y-yes," I replied as I blushed uncontrollably.

Diane worked to suppress a laugh and looked at her lover, placing her hand over his.

"Well, I'll leave that up to Eugene, but I think you should ask him, and nicely."

My blush deepened at the same rate as my cock hardened. I cleared my throat again and realized the problem. My pride was stuck in my throat. I had to swallow it.

"Eugene," I started, searching for words "May I watch?"

"Watch what?" My wife asked coyly. "What are you asking to watch?"

"You . . . him . . . as you . . . fuck." I spoke as I tried to organize my fevered brain.

Eugene's smile broadened as he patted my wife's hand affectionately.

"Why I think that's a fine idea, Jack," he stated indulgently. Then he leaned toward her, and they kissed.

"Dessert and then dessert," he said, and the statement made Diane giggle.

So, I served the dessert. Apple pie, freshly baked by me earlier in the day.

"Ice cream?" I asked Eugene, as I placed the pie before them. Eugene happily agreed.

"Mmmmm," Diane said, as she dug in. "Ice cream now, warm cream later." Her words caused them both to giggle this time and in fact made me chuckle if a little ruefully as I remembered the old saying: "It's funny because it's true."

ONCE THE FIRST DESSERT WAS CONSUMED, I cleared away the dishes and put them in the sink. At Diane's urging, I did not load the dishwasher. Amazingly enough, she was unwilling to delay her libidinous urges any longer. Even for the sake of a clean kitchen. So, we hurried to the bedroom and there, it was Eugene who was the "chef" cooking up his menu of debauchery, where the main course was my wife.

"Diane," he said, "stand beside the bed." Then looking at me, I was told, "Jack, undress your wife for me."

I did so without thinking, spurred on by my excitement. It was like unwrapping a present meant for someone else. As each item of clothing came off, their anticipation grew, until she was finally naked and stood under the watchful eyes of the huge black man who was the current focus of her carnal desires. At which point I thought my participation was ended.

At which point, I was wrong.

"Now," Diane said to me as she stood naked as the day she was born, "Undress Eugene for me."

The request startled me, mostly because it was not a request. It also was not a demand. More of an expectation. She knew I would comply, and so did he. They weren't wrong. I did, and I stepped toward a man with whom I had just eaten dinner, someone, with whom I'd had beers with earlier in the week. Who, Diane and I had eaten enchiladas accompanied by his wife. I unbuttoned his shirt and removed it. I was going to take it and hang it and he waved the effort off.

"No need, my friend," he told me. "Now the shoes." I bent and removed the very expensive loafers and his socks as my wife watched intently. I had yet to unwrap her "present" but she knew that was next, as placing his socks inside his shoes I reached for his belt. Unbuckling it, I unbuttoned his slacks and let them drop around his ankles. He stepped out and I put them off to the side, and kneeling back up, was faced with his dark undershorts and the obscene bulge they sought to contain. Behind me, I heard the woman I loved draw in a long breath as I took hold of the elastic waistband and lowered them, and his cock popped out. Long, hard, tubular intimidation. Seeing it made my skin crawl, but my own tiny member twitched in nervous excitement. Behind me, I heard," Ooooh," and as he stepped out of his shorts I moved out of the way. I was in my seat in the cuckold chair when Eugene spoke.

"Feel free to jerk off," he told me. "Won't bother us a bit." Then, having outlined my masturbation privileges, Eugene and Diane embraced and kissed, deeply and passionately as his hands went to the tight half-moons of her ass and he lifted her. She wrapped her arms around his well-muscled torso and dug her nails into the mahogany-colored skin of his back as he gently placed her on the bed. Then, when she was on her back with her legs raised, he went between them and began to feast on her soaking mound, which elicited low, animalistic sounds from her, and she mewled and squealed and soon came close to howling at the moon. She thrashed wildly trying to grind herself onto his skilled tongue until she was frantic with desire.

"Fuck me," she told him, "Fuck me, please." Her tone bordered on desperation, so, lifting his torso, he accommodated her wish, entering her in one swift stroke, which, considering the girth of his cock was amazing in and of itself. She cried out, but in pleasure not in pain and he buried himself deep in her and ground his hips, triggering an even more volcanic response. I had heard my wife in the throes of sexual ecstasy when Dan was "with us." Never in all her time being fucked by him did she reach the decibel level she did with Eugene that night. That fact alone made me like him more than I already did, as I took his suggestion and pulled my cock through my fly and began to stroke myself. Diane wailed and mewled and beseeched her creator as the long black cock pounded her mercilessly. As always, the sounds she made fueled my excitement and, whether, by luck or happy accident, I orgasmed at almost the same time my wife and her lover came, the three of us together, in stereophonic sound. We all lay in place, physically and mentally spent until finally, Eugene raised himself up off Diane and I realized that while my cum may have gone on the floor in front of me, Eugene's had gone into my wife. As he withdrew and a long string of cum drained out onto the bedsheets from his bare cock. He looked at me and said, "Can you get me a towel, Jack?" The look on my face and my response, which was to say, "Uhh." Must have tipped him off that I was surprised he hadn't worn a condom, something I had not noticed in the heat of the moment. Nevertheless, I recovered my senses enough to go to the bathroom and grab a towel and bring it back so he could completely extricate his member.

"Thanks, buddy," Eugene said graciously, and he put the towel under his dick and pulled out. Diane groaned unhappily when he did, and a flood of semen spilled out onto the bath towel.

"Oh, and no worries about the whole bareback thing," he told me.

"Yes, honey," Diane finally arose from her supine position and propped herself up on her elbow. "I got tested this week and so did Eugene."

"And, in case you wondered about an accidental pregnancy, I've been fixed," he said easing my other concern. After he said it, he added, "Can you imagine what Gayle would do to me if women started showing up at the house with little Eugenes and little Eugenies?" That made us all laugh as I self-consciously tucked myself back in and Eugene stood and pulled on his underpants and asked, "Is there any more of that pie left?"

# 4

"**A**ND DONALD IS GOING TO MEET us for drinks Wednesday?" Diane asked me over coffee about a man I'd never met, whom we would bring back to our home to fuck her brains out. She asked as casually as if she wondered if I'd made her an appointment at the dentist. Same principle, I supposed. In both instances, she'd get "drilled" though one would be more fun than the other. for her at least.

"Yes," I confirmed, "At Delmonico's West at 7."

She was putting on her coat to leave for work. As she did, she smiled.

"You'll like Donald," she told me. Donald was another of the men she'd met at Dan's Monday Night Football party. "He has a huge cock." I looked at her blankly and she looked back. As usual, she knew what I was thinking.

"Well," she said heading out the door. "Maybe you will like him despite that." Then she stopped and turned back to me as she headed out to the garage. "But, I will certainly like him because of that. Now come here and give me a kiss. Juris prudence waits for no one."

FINALLY, WEDNESDAY WAS UPON US AND we were seated in the bar at Delmonico's West with the well-endowed Donald. Thankfully, what my wife considered his "best quality" was hidden beneath a pair of well-worn jeans, though not hidden entirely as there was a considerable bulge in the crotch. It caught the eye of our server, Jaime. Jaime was male, nonetheless, Donald didn't seem put off by it. Perhaps appreciation was simply appreciation to some.

"So, Donald what do you do?" I asked because Diane could tell me not very much about our drinking companion, other than he was a white guy, in good shape and gorgeous. "Your height, but not your length," she had said. Cutting but accurate. Donald looked mid-twenties and if so, was much younger than her other liaisons had been. He was clean-shaven, except for what I had heard was termed a "soul patch," a small bit of a beard under his lower lip. I thought it looked ridiculous. I wondered if I told him that if it would hurt the mood. Seeing the woman, I loved moon over him made me think it would not.

"I work in a cycle shop," Donald replied sipping his beer, Budweiser. Truly, Donald was a man of the people. I simply nodded. Motorcycles had never held much attraction for me. I preferred cars. I wanted more steel around me than under me. Traveling at high rates of speed with so little covering you seemed reckless Though, upon further reflection, it was probably less risky than what we'd been doing now for weeks on end. At least hotwifing didn't put you in the line of fire of a careless semi-driver. Not that one could not get run over. It was more injurious to the ego than the body, at least so far.

I was getting hungry, whether or not anyone else was. So, I ordered the appetizer platter as my wife listened as Donald droned on about the inner workings of the "iron horse." My term, not his. It seemed appropriate, and Donald was the backend of that horse.

Diane was a good listener, which I attributed to her law school training. That talent served her well in her hotwifing quest for men, most of whom liked to talk, usually about themselves. Her tolerance for drivel seemed as epic as her appetite for sexual pleasure.

Two hours later that tolerance was rewarded as Donald delivered to her three orgasms that if not the most earth-shattering I had witnessed during my brief time as my wife's cuckold certainly seemed to satisfy her need. The last of them occurred with her riding Donald's long cock, cowgirl style, as she finally emitted a shrill scream and collapsed limply onto her new bull's slender, muscular chest.

After a brief rest period, the young man was politely, but summarily dismissed with her lying in bed and kissing him in what seemed to me to be a faux passion, after which I showed him to the door with a promise to call him "next time Diane's available."

"He's alright," was my wife's rather tepid comment.

"Next week?" I asked. She wanted to get everyone on a regular schedule, and I had been appointed her social secretary, in charge of debaucherous meetings. She waved her hand in a noncommittal fashion.

"Let's see who else comes along," was her reply. "Nate and Bradley still need to be scheduled."

Leaning against the doorjamb, I watched as my beautiful wife stretched her lithe naked body on the now despoiled bed sheets.

"You will handle that, won't you, dear?" She said it as a question, which it was not. It might have annoyed me once, the idea that I would arrange my wife's liaisons with disparate men. Now, it made me smile, that after our time with Dan I had some measure of control, however small.

"Yes dear," I said in response to the nonquestion. "And remember you'll have Eugene on Friday night. Gayle has a night out with her sister."

My wife turned on her side away from me and buried her head in her pillow.

"TMI," she stated flatly. "I have no interest in what Gayle's doing while her husband is doing me." Then, having said that she seemed to fall asleep, while I repaired to the bathroom to resume what had become my program of nonstop self-abuse.

# 5

As we went through what Diane termed, "entrance interviews" a hierarchy began to form. Eugene was presently in the lead, having the best combination of equipment and technique. Donald had youthful energy of his side, and a long, strong cock. However, his skills had yet to develop as fully as his endowment. My wife had a notion that it might be fun to be the sexy MILF to train this boy. CooCooCachoo Mrs. Robinson. Two more, Nate and Bradley, were yet to be tested.

Nate was another black man, of moderate height and build. Taller and stronger than me, but not so buff as Dan, nor as primal as Eugene. Then there was Bradley, a fortyish surfer dude stranded in the Midwest with nary an ocean in sight. He was slender and yet strong looking. Not as though he lifted weights, but like a runner.

Having checked with both, I penciled in Bradley first. only based on availability. He and Diane would meet at our house. Diane had gotten to know Bradley through Dan, during what could be most politely described as "get-togethers" at his penthouse apartment, but to use the vernacular were gang bangs.

We met Bradley on a Tuesday night. He came straight to the house since Diane had to work late and she was anxious to get to the "main event."

"Can we trust him?" I asked. My wife gave me the look that indicated she thought I was a moron, so I withdrew the question. Because of her schedule, I told him to be at our house at 8 p.m. At 8:35 we were still waiting.

"Are you sure you told him 8?" She asked it as she gave me the moron look again. I winced and replied that I had.

"When you told me you would be home at 6:30 I knew you needed at least an hour and a half to get ready," I explained. "That made 8."

She shook her head.

"For Bradley, I probably didn't need to get as ready as I would for another man," she said, "He's pretty laid back."

That much was evident from the pics she showed me. Longish blonde hair, t-shirts, and jeans, and or shorts. He was a waiter at one of the restaurants Dan, Diane's previous Bull, owned and when we spoke, he made it clear we needed to keep his involvement on the "down low." Keeping this whole messy affair on the down low was my goal. Sometimes I succeeded, but mostly I did not. So, I eagerly agreed. The only other thing he let me know was he drank tequila. I breathed a sigh of relief. My scotch was safe.

FINALLY, AT A QUARTER OF NINE, I heard a vehicle pull into the drive. Going to the door, I peeked out the side window and saw a battered truck parked and a blonde-haired man bound out and hurdle up the steps. I opened the door before he could ring the bell. As he came in, we exchanged pleasantries and a bit of small talk until Diane appeared and raised her wrist to look at her watch. Both of us sensed her impatience and Bradley went to her as I hung back and (as usual) watched. They embraced and kissed. I could feel the heat across the room. The delicious frisson caused by the collision of passion and need. Finally, the kiss broke and hand in hand the pair hurried to our bedroom and the clothes began to fly in all directions until both were naked. As for me, I went to my chair in the corner, to watch and to be assiduously ignored as the surfer dude threw my wife down on our bed and spread her legs with his hands, and without as much as a moment of foreplay, entered her waiting pussy, in one savage shove and began pounding her as hard he could, grunting from the effort as she cried out in what I took to be a combination of pain and pleasure. Her body rocked like a ragdoll under his brutal assault, then sprang to life in a flurry of swearwords that would make a longshoreman blush, until, suddenly, it ended, and Bradley withdrew. He took hold of his cock and peeled off the condom, depositing it in the wastebasket I had placed beside the bed. Once that was safely disposed of, Diane drew him to her and they kissed again. This time the kiss was not volcanic, but friendly. Then he picked up his clothes and redressed as I watched, and Diane lay back and pulled the sheet over her still naked body. Once dressed he said goodbye to me and left, hesitating a moment as though expecting a tip. What he got was thanks for coming. As he left, I looked at my ravished wife in our bed and all I could think was:

"I bought two bottles of tequila for this?"

# 6

**I**T WAS A FRIDAY MORNING AND we were sitting drinking coffee and discussing mundane things when Diane gave me the news:

"Dana's pregnant."

I nodded and took another sip of coffee, unaffected by the news that my young sister-in-law and her similarly young husband were "in the family way," as they used to say in old movies and sitcoms. However, what my wife said next made me react with a typical sitcom response.

"It's not Sean's," Diane said it as matter of factly, as if she had said it was snowing outside or we needed milk. Upon hearing that I did a "spit take," spraying coffee all over the counter and some on Diane's robe. Taking a tea towel, I wiped the counter and then dabbed at her terry cloth-covered breasts. She took the towel and swatted my hand away, clearly annoyed.

"It's not . . ." I said started to ask and let the question dangle. My wife nodded.

"It is," she confirmed. "You are quite the little matchmaker," she declared, placing the towel off to the side. "The rabbit died and they may have killed it, but you got the bunny boiling."

Taking Diane's cup and my own I went to the coffee maker and gave us each a refill, then doctored hers up so it was unrecognizable as coffee except for the latent caffeine.

"Thanks, honey," she smiled and took a sip as I sat back on the stool beside her.

"I feel bad," I confessed.

"You should you home wrecker, you," she looked and me and frowned slightly, and shook her head.

"Don't feel too bad," she told me. "She has been wanting a baby since they got married. Sean wasn't getting the job done."

I knew Dana and her husband had not been meshing sexually from what she'd said the day we had "coffee" together. What I didn't know is that she was looking for a sperm donor as much as a "boy toy." If I had known that my decision might have been different. Considering the result was getting Diane's former bull out of our lives and out of my bed with my wife in it, well, maybe not.

"Did she . . ." I began then realized I didn't know how to phrase the question. "Was it on purpose?" Diane shrugged.

"She says not," was her answer. "I don't know. I have my doubts."

Me too. Diane had been "cock struck" by the handsome muscleman. Dana was positively smitten. In the one instance that we had seen them together since Diane ended her involvement, she was embarrassingly so, openly displaying affection, even in the presence of her and Diane's mother. Sean, for his part, seemed to not be distressed by another man being overly familiar with his wife in public. Despite his frequent business trips, the young couple didn't seem to have much "welcome home sex, "at least according to Diane. More than that, it was as though it was Dana's chance to rest from the constant amorous activity of which I knew Dan was capable. Activities that had produced Dana's pregnancy.

"Does Sean know she's . . . you know." I asked carefully, unsure how to say it delicately.

"Not yet," Diane replied shaking her head. "She's trying to figure out how to tell him. Mostly because he'll know it's not his."

My wife's response made me widen my eyes in shock and begged another question.

"Why?"

"They haven't had sex in months," she told me. "Of any kind, but especially the kind that leads to knitting baby booties."

She drained her coffee cup and placed it back on the counter before her.

"In fact, you, my dear husband have had more recent intimate contact with my sister's coochie than Sean." Having said that, she smiled and got off her stool.

"Can you toast me a bagel, honey?" Diane asked. "I need to move my ass and get dressed. I have a client at 10."

LITTLE MORE THAN HALF AN HOUR later, in what may have been a world speed record for her dressing, she came back into the kitchen. So quick was she that her bagel was still toasting. Once it popped up, I slathered it with cream cheese and handed it to her with a napkin. She smiled and leaned over to kiss me lightly, so as not to smear her lipstick. Before she turned to leave, I felt a need to ask a question.

"Are you jealous?" I asked my wife who looked at me in surprise.

"Of . . . ?" She said back to me questioningly.

"Dana," I explained. "Being pregnant."

Diane instantly made a face and emitted a sound I interpreted to indicate disgust. Looking at me she shook her head.

"God, no," She declared. Her answer filled me with a sense of relief. She spread both hands and said, "Why would I want to ruin this body? Why would I want to get fat?" She said it and opened the door to the garage, taking with her the bagel I had made, thick with cream cheese to eat on the way to work.

EUGENE ARRIVED AT THE HOUSE AT 7 on Friday and the evening settled into a pattern that for me had become comfortable and familiar. Diane and he repaired to the bedroom and fucked while I cooked. I was roasting a prime rib and the last thing I wanted was for it to be overdone. The noises from the bedroom seemed somehow "muted," so I wondered if they had closed the door this time. Stepping away from the stove, I looked down the hall. The door was open, but the sounds seemed less excited than usual, especially from my wife. I went back to where I was sautéing green beans in garlic and white wine and wondered if something was wrong. Strangely enough, I was not wondering what was wrong with a man who listens and watches as another man fucks his wife. I had resolved that question within myself a while back, deciding it was the price I had to pay for having a gorgeous, sexy wife whom I could not satisfy. Adding in what seemed to be a naturally masochistic nature on my part, provided the answer. It was perhaps not satisfying but was at least an answer.

Dinner went on as it had the previous nights, with Eugene enjoying my cooking and with my wife enjoying embarrassing me, by again asking me to thank her Bull and him telling me it was his pleasure (because everyone loves a funny Bull), and then me serving the dessert. Molten chocolate cakes this time. Then Eugene made his joke about "dessert and then dessert" (The funny Bull thing again). After which we adjourned to the bedroom, where things moved more hurriedly than usual. Not in a way that seemed to indicate they couldn't keep their hands off one another. Eugene seemed no less enthusiastic than he always was. Diane on the other hand gave the definite impression she wanted to do it and get it over with.

Which they did in under half an hour, at which time the big man dressed and excused himself, giving my wife a rather perfunctory kiss and shaking my hand and after we thanked each other telling me he knew his way out.

Something was wrong. I could feel it. Diane was laying sprawled out on the bed, so I went and lay beside her, and gently stroked her hair.

"Did you and Eugene have fun?" I began cautiously. Diane nodded but with no conviction.

My mind began to race, wondering what the problem might be. Had Gayle made her husband break it off? I had thought he was going to stay the weekend and he obviously was not. We were alone and as always, I was grateful when we were, but Diane's altered attitude was disquieting. Finally, after deciding I wasn't smart enough to figure out what was going on myself, I did what I normally didn't do with my wife. I asked a direct question.

"Something wrong Puddin?"

Diane lifted her arms and crossed them in front of her face, as I continued stroking her hair.

"Eugene's a nice man," she said from behind her crossed arms.

"Very nice," I agreed. When I said that, her response was to press her forearms into her face tighter.

"That's the problem," she finally admitted as she groaned.

"He's too fucking NICE!"

The statement struck me oddly. As I thought about it, it made a kind of sense. She had been introduced to the hotwife dynamic by a man who fucked her roughly, disregarded her feeling (not to mention mine), and in general treated her like a piece of meat. She had transitioned to a man who however well-endowed treated us both with respect and consideration. As per her plan, he was not the only man in her sex life, but the other two she'd had relations with, though sexy in their own ways could by no means be called commanding. This presented a challenge to my wife, and if I knew one thing about my wife when met with a challenge, she had always found a solution. So, I asked.

"So, what do you want to do?"

Without looking at me, I knew she was smiling as she said, "I have a solution."

See? Told ya so.

# 7

Later I found out the solution's name was "Deacon." His internet picture told me little other than he was a white guy who shaved his head and like Dan put in considerable gym time. When Diane showed me the picture, she didn't tell me very much about him, and I got the feeling it was not because she didn't know much. She let me know she had been talking to him for a while after having found him on the same site that gave us the inimitable Dan. All these factors worried me, but when I asked questions, she merely smiled and said, "I guess we will have to find out won't we?"

But before we could "find out" about Deacon we had a new prospective Bull scheduled.

"Should I cancel Tim?" I asked as I looked at the picture and short internet bio of the latest man of my wife's dreams, which Tim was obviously not. He was another of the men Diane had "met" at Dan's Monday Night Football debauching and seemed to not be one of the more exciting ones. She had contacted him when her other Bulls were otherwise occupied on a night she had planned on playing. Tim was a middle manager at a local pet food company. Maybe we'd at least get some free dog food out of it. Sadly, we did not have a dog. Someone to keep me company in the spare bedroom as random studs fucked my wife's brains out. Someone to lick my face and be happy I was home, and not happy because I was home making dinner and delivering drinks to her and her lovers, unlike my wife, who had not licked any part of me in a very long time. When Diane spoke of Tim's sexual technique (she volunteered. I was well past asking), she said he was "fine." When I pointed out that "fine" was for sandpaper, she told me she found the question "grating" and the jokes deteriorated from there. So, I prepared to host Tim.

TIM WAS COMING TO DINNER AS well as "dessert" (to borrow Eugene's metaphor). This was made more complicated when I discovered he was a vegan. I had never cooked for a vegan before and the fact that we were having a "meatless Monday" didn't please my wife, a noted carnivore. When I suggested we cancel, she said no.

"It might be good for us," she said with no conviction whatsoever. "Besides it's his meat I'm interested in and not the grocers."

The result of her sexual desperation was me scouring the internet for vegan recipes, none of which inspired much appetite in a man raised in the heart of cattle country. Finally, I stumbled upon one that seemed less nauseating than the rest, and noting the ingredients, went to the store and bought them and the meal preparation was well underway when Tim arrived at 6.

"Can I get you a drink?" I asked in the solicitous manner that I'd perfected since the start of this shitshow my wife embraced as hotwifing. Tim's response was one I was sure would not please Diane.

"I don't drink."

It didn't. After I had Tim seated in the living room with a sparkling water I went to tell my wife her ship had come in.

"He doesn't what?" Was the unpleased response I expected, though less profane than I would have guessed. I confirmed he was, to use an old phrase a "tea totaller." At that point she let me know, while she might eschew animal products to get laid, she would need a drink to do so. Or several and was dispatched to the bar to fetch her the first of those.

"How's your water, Tim?" I asked as I passed through the living room to the bar. He looked at the still mostly full glass.

"Okay, I guess."

As I assembled a scotch and soda for his paramour, I hoped that Tim's lovemaking style was more dynamic than his personality.

IT TURNED OUT, IT WAS. HIS cock was decently large and quite thick and (according to Diane) he knew how to use it. When they were done for the second time, Diane at least seemed happy and the unexpressive Tim dressed, said his goodbyes, and left us alone, at which point, I looked at my wife lying sprawled across our bed and tried to discern her mood.

"Was he . . . 'fine?'" I asked.

"The sex was . . . good," she said hesitantly.

"But not 'grate?'" I replied continuing the metaphor.

"His personality was 'grating'" Diane she responded looking thoughtful.

"He rubbed me the wrong way too." After I said it, we both laughed. Diane was smart. She was good at getting the joke. She was still chuckling when she grabbed the covers, pulled them over her, and rolled onto her side.

"Well," she began as she buried her face in her pillow. "Tomorrow I'm going to call Deacon. One thing's 'plane,' I need some new 'wood.'"

# 8

We took the next night off from sexual excess and by 8 p.m. had finished dinner and were seated on the couch together. Diane was on her phone with her sister. I was watching "The Mandalorian" with the sound low enough that she could hear what Dana was saying.

"So, how did Sean take the news?" I heard her ask. As the program played out on the large hi-def screen, the greater drama seemed to be my sister-in-law's pregnancy and its repercussions. So, I ignored baby Yoda in favor of eavesdropping on the baby story my wife was being told next to me on the couch.

"Really?" Diane exclaimed. She had on her earphones so I could hear only her side of the conversation, or as happened a few seconds later, see her covering the receiver to keep Dana from hearing as she giggled. "Oh, yes," she said as soon as she could speak again. "I'm sure he did." Then she held her empty glass out to me to wordlessly ask for a refill. Apparently, sisterly gossip was thirsty work. I took the tumbler from her and mixed another scotch and soda. Diane had developed a taste for Johnny Walker Blue which while making up for Dan no longer being there to drink it, left me with an overabundance of Grey Goose vodka, which she had been drinking while under his purview. It was an imbalance I welcomed, although I hoped we'd come across a bull who favored vodka to diminish the supply. I hurriedly mixed the drink, making it strong, like she liked her bulls, not weak like she liked her husband. By the time I rejoined her on the couch, she was off the phone, shaking her head. Handing her the glass, I looked at her expectantly hoping for an explanation. Before I got one, though she took a long pull of the golden mixture and smiled appreciatively.

"My sister," she said in a tone that indicated amazement. She shook her head again and took another drink.

"What?" I finally asked impatiently.

"Dana hasn't told Sean" she explained. "She told Dan."

I leaned back on the couch. The revelation stunned me, and I sat a moment and looked at Diane and she nodded, drained her glass, and held it out to me. Picking up my own I went back toward the bar. Now I needed a drink, though I was glad I hadn't had a mouthful of scotch when my wife told me. Another spit take would have surely earned me a smack or at least a night on the couch.

"My sister's life is an episode of Maury Povich," she said laughing, but it was a rueful laugh.

Finally, the inevitable question. I suspected the answer but had to ask.

"What did he say when she told him?"

Diane looked at me and scowled.

"What would you expect he'd say?" She said it sharply, with more than a hint of sarcasm. I knew exactly what Dan would say.

"He wished her good luck?" I said feebly. My wife nodded and sipped more scotch.

"Not even that," she said affirming my low opinion of her former bull, hers too.

"We had the chance, honey," she told me. "He was tied to the chair. All we needed was a sharp knife." It was a fantasy. Wish fulfillment. Something I myself had dreamed of doing for almost the whole time he and my wife were involved. It was a dream. Every guy's gotta have a dream. It was strangely reaffirming to realize Diane had the same dream.

Diane's sister was young, beautiful, and ruthless. She had always, in my experience, gotten what she wanted. It must have been jarring to realize she was not going to ride off into the sunset with the man she had stolen from her sister. To have his baby and build a white picket fence around his penthouse apartment. At least she still had her young successful husband. Sexually disinterested as he might be, he was a high achiever businesswise and a go-getter and on the fast track. The question now became would he raise a baby sired by another man? Also, another question remained, why would a young, healthy male ignore the carnal needs of an equally young sexy wife to the point that there was no possibility the baby she carried was his?

My wife saw the look on my face and instinctively knew the unasked question.

"Dana told me Sean's gay."

I GOT DIANE A TOWEL TO WIPE off the scotch I spit on her blouse after the revelation. Surprisingly, I was not banished to the spare room or couch after that faux pas. Once she was dried off, she explained to me what was going on.

"She suspected it when they were dating," she told me after I had refreshed both our drinks.

"But, he was so gorgeous and such a high achiever, she married him anyway."

I nodded to encourage her to continue, which she did.

"I guess she thought she would turn him around." She hesitated a bit then added, "So to speak."

I nodded again. Because well, when something is working for you stay with it, and also because I knew, where this might go.

"Certainly," she continued. "know how that is."

Ouch. She said it. She brought the elephant into the room and directed it to step on my... toe. Then, unfortunately, I felt the need to respond defensively.

"But, I'm not gay."

My wife smiled benevolently.

"No, dear, you are not," she said. "I realize that. But like my sister I married someone sexually . . . 'incompatible' in hopes that would change. It didn't. So, I changed it. So did she. Ironically in the same way."

"With the same man," I added without thinking. The comment made Diane wince.

"Yes," she replied sourly. "But she had help."

Now it was my turn to wince.

The awkwardness was broken up when a message beeped into Diane's phone. I assumed It was another from her sister. Her response told me it was not. She laughed. Not a mirthful laugh, not a giggle. It was an evil laugh.

"Deacon's coming over Saturday night," she informed me. "He's telling me what we need to do to be ready."

# 9

"**C**AN YOU DRAW MY BATH, DARLING, and make me a drink?"

My wife used a rather solicitous tone when she said it, but I knew it was really not a request.

"Don't you think it's a little early, honey?" I asked. We had started earlier on other days, but today was Saturday. Deacon was coming tonight and unlike Tim, Diane let me know he did drink, and she certainly intended to. She looked at me with her withering gaze. The one that broke witnesses down under cross-examination. It broke me down too, as while I prepared to retreat to the bar, she added dismissively, "It's five o'clock somewhere."

When I returned with her Scotch and soda, Diane was standing at the edge of the tub as it filled. I had started the process before I went to fulfill my wife's needs for spirits. She was wrapped in her fluffy white robe. She turned as I entered and took the tumbler from me, taking a long sip of the amber liquid. Placing the glass on the side of the tub, she untied the robe and turned her back to me, which I took as her desire for me to help her remove it. Which I did, hanging it on the door and looking at her as she stood naked. She reached her hand to me. Taking it, I helped her into the warm water. She sat and then lay back and her breasts floated invitingly as I watched her settle in. It was a large tub, and when we first bought the house, there were many times when we bathed in it together. That was a lifetime ago or so it seemed. I was not invited in, though Diane's next statement indicated she felt I needed to start preparing for our guest.

"You need to shower," she told me, though as with her drinking, I thought it might be early. Be that as it may, I started to pull off my shirt to use the master bath's separate shower stall.

"Can you use the guest bath, Jack?" She asked as she played with the bubbles that dotted the surface of her bathwater. "Oh, and I left something in there for you. Use it please."

I looked at her and was assiduously ignored, so I went to the guest bath, a place I had become familiar with using during Dan's reign of terror. Sliding back the shower curtain, I saw there was a bottle on the shelf, alongside the body wash and shampoo. I picked it up and read it. I was shocked when I realized it was depilatory. I read it again, struggling with the idea. Then I took it back to the master bath to get an explanation from my wife.

"Depilatory?" I asked in confusion. Diane smiled at me.

"Yes, It's something I've thought about for a long time," she explained as she splashed some bathwater on her breasts seductively. "You'll be so smooth and sexy. Yummy. I'll want to eat you right up if you do it."

I looked at my wife and looked back at the bottle and given the twisted state of my mind it made perfect sense. So, without another word, I retreated back to the guest bath where I showered and reading the instruction on the bottle, proceeded to remove my body hair. Luckily enough, it was sparse, and once the chemical depilatory had cleared most of it, the scraper that was provided with the hair removal kit, rid me of most of the rest. Whatever that didn't get I took off with the razor I used to shave my face, which I did, and soon I was smooth as a snake all over.

"Are you done?" I heard my wife call from the other room. "I'm ready to get out." Throwing on my bathrobe, I hurried to where

Diane was shivering in the bathwater, which had by then gone cold. She held out her hand and I helped her out of the tub. As she stood dripping on the bathmat I handed her a towel, which she handed back.

"Dry me, please," she said. The please, was gratuitous but I began to gently dab at her saturated flesh. Touching her body in such intimate ways never ceased exciting me. Finally, she was dry and I placed her robe back on her and she wrapped herself into it snuggly. Once she had retied the belt, she turned.

"Let me see."

I let the bathrobe slide off my shoulders and fall to the floor and stood trembling slightly as my wife closely examined my naked and now hairless body. Her fingers felt my groin where my pubes had been and as she did my cock stirred and hardened. She paid no attention other than to go, "Hmmph" and tell me to turn. Once I faced away from her, she ran her hands over my back and down my torso to my ass. Parting the cheeks, she felt between them. Then I heard her go, "Aha." Then a pinch and a pulling and a sharp pain, after which she held a single hair so I could see.

"You missed one," she told me and I smiled weakly. She smiled back and deposited the hair in the wastebasket and continued her inspection, going down my legs and then my feet.

Finally, she stood and took my shoulders and looked me in the eye and smiled.

"Now," she said, "Let's go finish getting ready."

"You're getting really good at that, honey," She told me as I spread smooth coats of clear lacquer on each of her toes.

"Thanks," I replied trying not to allow talking to distract me from the task at hand. "It's not a talent I thought I would ever develop."

My wife giggled at the admission.

"Well, now at least you have one useful skill," She told me mockingly, which made me look up at her away from her pinky toe.

"I'll remember that the next time I make you a drink," I replied ruefully. My retort made her pick up her glass and drain the entrails.

"Speaking of which honey," she said "Can you get me another?" I was finishing the last toe when she asked it, so I carefully placed her foot down and headed toward the bar, to employ one of my other "useful skills." as I departed the bathroom, she told me to get one for myself.

"You might need it."

IN FACT, I NEEDED TWO, WHEN I found the direction the night was headed, which started out with me painting my toenails. Not the clear polish I had applied to my wife's, but a soft, demure pink.

"Coral," Diane corrected me as I blew on the polish to help it dry. Looking at my feet she declared them "perfect," then took my hands and glued on long fake fingernails. The color matched that of my toes.

Once the last one was applied, I squeezed my hand together and tried to make a fist. I found I could not, though I did then realize if I got in a fight like this, I could scratch my opponent's eyes out.

I had asked twice and been ignored, but I tried again.

"Why are we doing this?" Diane just smiled.

"Because I bought all these lovely things," she went to the closet and brought out a hanger with a bra hanging on it, still tagged. It was the same coral pink as my nails and toes, and I had the sneaking suspicion it was not meant for her to wear.

"Try this on," she said holding the lacey garment toward me. Instead, I recoiled.

"Why would I want to do that?" I asked incredulously, as I looked at the bra like it was a poisonous snake.

"Because I'd love it if you did," she told me as she smiled sweetly. We looked at each other and I knew she was bringing to bear all the powers her womanly wiles and her Ivy league legal training could muster, and that in the end, I would succumb to either or both. I took the hanger from her, holding it delicately, in just my thumb and index finger, and regarded it warily.

"Well," I said resignedly, "you're going to have to show me how to put this thing on."

Diane giggled and wasted no time pulling the bra free of its hanger and ripping off the tags, wrapping it around me, and fastening it. It was a strapless design so that made the process simpler. She pushed at the cups, which lay flat against my chest.

"Oh." she said snapping her fingers, "I forgot." With that, she ran to her closet and came back with what looked like two cone-shaped sponges. She pulled the cups away from my body one at a time, inserted the spongey, coney things, then pushed and adjusted till their positioning suited her. Once she had them where she wanted, she stepped away and admired her work.

"There. Boobs for the boobless," she said smirking at her own joke.

I looked down. I didn't smirk. I wasn't amused. I didn't joke. I was horrified. I looked down, stepped to the side in front of the full-length mirror, and felt like crying.

"I have breasts," I wailed plaintively. My distress seemed to amuse my wife even more than my changed appearance. She turned me and we hugged, our boobs pressing together awkwardly. Then she leaned back and held me at arm's length. She wanted to say something. I knew she did. Then unfortunately for me, she said it.

"Honey, let me be the first to say . . . you've never looked better."

# 10

"**H**OLD STILL, OR I'LL SMEAR YOUR MASCARA," Diane told me as I leaned to her so she could apply color to my eyes, which she minutes before described as "bland."

"There." She declared, satisfied with the result of her effort. Moving aside, she allowed me to see myself. My reaction was not satisfaction, it was shock. The face looking back at me was not mine. The face looking back was painted with gaudy makeup liberally applied, so much so as to give a freakish image. A caricature of femininity, a freak.

Diane went to her closet and brought something back. I was too busy staring at the woman in the mirror to notice what it was.

"Arms up," I was told and she slipped something over my head, blocking my vision and momentarily stopping my fixation with my painted face. She stood between me and the mirror and tugged and adjusted the garment until the fit seemed "right." Then she stepped aside so I could see what I was wearing to host her new Bull.

It was at that point that I screamed and then moaned in shame at what I had become and in dread at what it implied was to come.

What she had dressed me in was . . . a dress. Or more specifically a uniform.

"A maid's uniform?" I asked in the most outraged tone I could manage looking as I then looked.

"French maid," my wife corrected. "Tonight, you will be Jaqueleen."

She pulled the dress down in front to expose more of my foam-enhanced chest.

"Deacon wanted you to be 'Fifi,' but I said no, Jaqueleen would be more fitting."

I frowned at the explanation, but my displeasure was as usual ignored.

"I thought you said I didn't have the legs for an outfit like this," I said, trying to use her own words to get me out of this particular humiliation. My ruse was destined to fail as she went once more to her closet and came back carrying hose and shoes.

"But first," she said holding wide and low a garment with which I was too familiar, "Step into these." I did and she pulled the lacey g-string up till it was between my cheeks and the satiny front covered my cock which had, despite my shame become fully engorged during this process. Once the undies were securely in place, she told me to sit on the edge of the bed, which I did. Then she rolled sheer white stockings onto my newly smooth legs and secured them with a garter belt she placed around my waist. Once those were on, she had me stand and step into the shoes, which were the same pale pink as my uniform and had very high heels. I teetered on them for a few seconds and she encouraged me to take a step. Then another, until I found my balance, which was what walking in high heels required along with strong legs. I had those, thanks to riding our Peloton daily. So, once I could stand and step, she had me walk across the room.

"Move your hips," my wife said coaching me. Then after a few trips, she seemed pleased.

Then she went back into her closet, emerging with the final detail.

"A wig?" I whined pathetically. Diane had me sit so she could fit me with a skull cap, after which she placed the wig and adjusted it appropriately. I looked in the mirror and was horrified and yet at the same time fascinated. My hair was blonde, and the cut was short, yet very stylish. The sort of cut I would have admired, on someone else. Specifically, a female someone else.

"Why blonde?" I asked. My wife grinned at me.

"Because blondes have more fun, silly," she replied giggling.

"That's it, Jacquleen" She declared proudly. "Now, let's get me ready."

I had gotten used to getting my wife ready for other men and had become good at it. This night was different, and it started with her makeup which was understated and discreet. Less even than she would wear to her office.

She was still in her bathrobe as we applied her sparse makeup. Once she had the effect, she wanted she got up from her makeup chair and went to her closet and returned with lingerie. White, and a dress, also white. She laid the dress on the bed and handed me the bra and panty set. I took it as she dropped her robe off her shoulders and stood naked and magnificent, waiting for me to dress her.

First was the bra, and as soon as it was on there was a noticeable difference from those my wife usually wore, even at work. It fully encompassed her luscious breasts, leaving less than a hint of cleavage. Then she stepped into the panties, which weren't granny panties but close.

Once both items were on, Diane looked and turned different angles and nodded and smiled, and then motioned toward the dress.

The first thing I noticed was there was a lot of fabric. Again, more even than she would ordinarily wear to court or the office. I lifted it over her head and settled it on her shoulders and then it was my turn to push and pull and tug till everything was in its proper place.

It was a knee-length dress, maybe slightly lower, and rode high on her bosom. It was beyond discreet and less revealing than what she had worn when she won the big judgment against a local power company. This dress was much different than that though. That outfit sent a message that she didn't have to show her body because she was powerful in ways that went beyond seduction. This dress gave the opposite impression. One of innocence.

Once I had dressed her, she pulled her hair back and did something with it I had never seen her do. She put her luxurious blonde hair into two pigtails. She could not have looked different than the power attorney or the femme fatale I was used to, and I hated to admit that I liked it. She caught me staring.

"Don't you have something to do?" She asked leadingly. I did and left without speaking to go to the kitchen, as fast as my high-heeled feet would carry me. There I took out of the fridge two platters of hor oeuvres I had assembled previously and put them in the preheated oven. Then I busily minced around the kitchen getting plates and glasses then setting the bar up so all was in readiness for my wife's "guest."

Not too long after that, the front doorbell rang. The sound made me jump. Perhaps because of memories of what had been happening lately after the bell rang. I looked toward the door and saw a silhouette in the frosted glass. A dark visage. He rang again, but instead of answering the door, I hurried to the bedroom where my wife was still working on her look.

"I think he's here," I told her. She looked at me blankly.

"You . . . think?" She asked. "Why don't you let him in?"

The thought terrified me.

"What if it isn't him?" I said, "Suppose it's Jamie next door, wanting to borrow a cup of sugar?"

Diane looked at me in a way that combined amusement and contempt in equal measure.

"Well, for god's sake don't give her my sugar," she said, "Give her that bleached shit, Dan liked. Now go. Shoo."

Having been given my orders I turned and left her, while she was still attempting to look demure to answer the door for someone who was probably not a neighbor looking for sugar, but a man I'd never met who wanted to borrow a cup of my wife.

# 11

Being a perceptive sort, I knew as soon as I opened the door it was not the neighbor.

"Good evening," I said in greeting because frankly, I didn't know what else to say. "Won't you come in . . . Sir?" The "Sir" part was extemporaneous. A holdover from my Dan days, but it felt right.

"I'm Deacon," he told me as he strode in. "But I imagine you already guessed that, didn't you?"

The comment made me laugh just a little.

"Well, I knew you weren't a neighbor coming over to borrow a cup of sugar," I replied, "by the way, I'm Jack . . . queleen." I averted my eyes from his penetrating gaze as I said it.

Deacon came dressed to make a statement. He wore a black leather trench coat, black jeans and boots, and a black long-sleeved t-shirt that fit tightly over his muscular torso. As in the picture I had seen, his head was shaved and it gleamed as though it was polished. My response made him smile and nod appreciatively as he looked me up and down.

"Can I take your coat, Sir?" As I asked, I noticed that he was carrying a sizable overnight bag, so he was obviously going to be with us a while. Deacon nodded, shrugged off the leather coat, and handed it to me. I hung it carefully in the hall closet and led him to the living room.

"Have a seat in here Sir. Diane will be here very soon," I used my most obsequious tone as I also asked, "Can I get you a drink?"

"You can Jacqueleen," he replied. "Vodka, Grey Goose if you have it."

Suppressing my inner "Huzzah" I merely smiled at Deacon and told him that yes, I believed we did have some of that particular brand. After being informed he took his over ice, I minced away with all deliberate speed toward the bar.

DEACON WAS WELL INTO HIS DRINK when Diane finally emerged.

"Good evening, Deacon," she said in a shy, reticent way I had not ever heard from her in the four years I had known her. She was radiant in her white dress, seeming as ladylike as always, but somehow more... modest. Seemingly gone was the powerful attorney, replaced by a shy and timorous, dare I say, virginal girl.

Deacon, smiled and nodded. His smile was wolfish as he watched her attempt at innocence. Finally, I stirred from the trance watching them induced and went to the bar and mixed the drink I knew my wife would want. I carried the tumbler of scotch and soda as carefully as was possible in six-inch heels, only to have Deacon wave me away.

"She will take a white wine," I was told by the man in black. "Do you have a sauvignon blanc?"

I assured him I did and hurried back to the bar to bring her what he had wanted my wife to have. Once I was out of sight, I took a long pull from the rejected drink. I'd always loved scotch and hated scotch and soda. Waste not want not, I'd always said. After I had drained the glass by half, I went to the wine cooler in search of the wine Deacon had ordered.

When I returned, they were still sitting silently. Deacon watching closely, Diane seemingly uncomfortable being watched.

"You can serve the hors d'oeuvres Jaqueleen," he said without looking at me. So, away I went, got the food out of the oven where it had been warming. After placing it on trays I delivered to my wife and her Bull.

I retreated after serving them and observed them from the kitchen. Deacon drank and ate slowly, deliberately. Diane sipped her white wine delicately and ate not at all, which was not like her. She sat and sipped in what appeared to be a caricature of virginal femininity. All the while watching him apprehensively. Anticipating . . . what?

Then, once he placed his empty glass on the side table and had eaten the last appetizer on his plate, the man in black showed us, the what.

"Jacquelleen," he called to me, "bring me my satchel, please." Deacon hadn't raised his voice when he said it, but as I passed them to go to where the bag was still sitting where he had left it in the hall, I saw my wife tremble. It was slight but noticeable and was a reaction I did not interpret as lust, but fear. I walked back the leather satchel to him and he took it, thanking me.

"You're . . . welcome?" I said smiling a thin, polite smile. He didn't look up, as he was busy rummaging for what he sought. When he withdrew the long wooden object, Diane drew in a sharp breath and I stared in stunned amazement.

It was a paddle.

"You made me wait," Deacon said to Diane in a calm stern tone. "Was it right to make me wait?"

My normally headstrong wife dropped her eyes to the floor, unwilling to look at the man who had come there at her request. He asked again.

"Was it nice to make me wait?"

Finally, Diane's head shook slightly and she said quietly, "No Deacon. It was not nice."

Deacon nodded and pointed to the arms of the sofa.

"Lay across that," he said calmly, but firmly. "Don't make a move or a sound."

"Yes, Deac . . ."

"Uh, uh," he corrected her. "That's a sound."

Diane settled herself across the sofa's arm, and Deacon reached down and pulled the dress up exposing her white pantied bottom. Then he turned to me.

"Come here and roll down your wife's panties," he said, "Please?" He stopped me as I approached and took me aside and whispered in my ear.

"You need to trust me," he said quietly. "Whatever happens. You can trust that I may hurt Diane, but I will not harm her."

He placed a hand on my bare shoulder.

"Do you trust me?" He asked. Thinking, I reached deep down into myself. Knowing the risks, but also knowing how intelligent my wife was I decided if she wanted this, then she obviously trusted this man. If she trusted him, I trusted him. So, I nodded. He patted me and smiled.

"If at any time you hear her say 'RED,' I will stop. That's her safe word, Not 'NO,' not 'STOP,' not, 'THAT HURTS LIKE A MOTHERFUCKER.' Red. We discussed all this before I ever came here." He told me in the same hushed tones and when he finished, he turned back to Diane as I knelt behind her and rolled the white panties down and exposed her pale and perfect asscheeks.

"My paddle please," he asked politely indicating the wood plank he had removed from his case. Handing it to him, I stepped back. Deacon rubbed the smooth polished surface of the wooden implement, then reached down and did the same to my wife's ass. His touch made her jump. Her response made the Bull smile, though she could not see it. The hem of her dress was over her head. She couldn't see him hold the paddle up, she couldn't see him aim carefully. She couldn't see him swing paddle toward her naked and exposed derriere.

She did, however, feel the impact. The paddle landed with a loud whacking sound and as it did, Diane cried out. My instincts made me want to go to her, to stop him from hurting her, but I did not, as I heard Deacon chide her, " That's a sound." Then add, "But you are allowed to say one thing. You are allowed to count each stroke. I didn't hear you say that the one you just got was ONE, so I guess that was what . . . a practice swing?"

"ONE," Diane cried out in a tone verging on panic, "ONE, ONE, ONE!"

Deacon laughed, and said, "There's my good girl. Yes, that's one." Having said that he pulled back the paddle and brought it down on Diane's reddened ass with great force. I heard her grunt, but he didn't correct her so I guessed a grunt must not be considered a sound in Deacon's world. After the grunt, she choked out, "TWO!" past gritted teeth, then THREE and FOUR, and FIVE, all accompanied by grunts. After the fifth blow, he placed the paddle off to the side and looked at me again.

"This is the point at which we do what's called aftercare," he explained. "Usually, I would do it, but in this case, I think it's more appropriate that you do it. Get in there and comfort your wife."

So, I went to where Diane was bent over the couch arm and kissed her reddened and painfully bruised ass, doing everything I could to soothe her orally, then once that seemed done, I took her in my arms and held her tenderly. She rested her face against my shoulder, which because of the cut of the maid's outfit was bare, so I felt a few tears. Then she sniffled and drew back, looking up at Deacon.

"Thank you," she said softly. To him, not me. She then released her hold on me and stood and they embraced and kissed, passionately, for a long time as I sat awkwardly in my pink French maid's costume with the white silk stockings and the six-inch heels. As I watched I realized something. Two somethings actually. I felt hurt and jealous as hell. Though I should have been used to seeing my wife express her sexuality in my presence with other men, I had not. The other realization was that my cock, small though it was, had escaped its satin g-string and was poking its little head out of the crinoline under my short skirt.

Finally, their kissing ceased and they looked at each other longingly.

"Shall we?" Deacon asked Diane.

"Let's," my wife replied. She took his hand and they headed toward the hall. I knew their destination was my bedroom. Deacon called to me over his shoulder to bring his bag and come along.

I did.

# 12

Once in the bedroom, Deacon attached leather straps to each corner of the bed frame. He then buckled wrist and ankle cuffs to each strap. Once those were in place, he went back to his satchel and brought out various implements of punishment that made the paddle he had used pale in comparison. Whips, crops, clamps, and chains, all in that one overnight bag. It was like a clown car until he had it completely unpacked and the contents spread out in an array of intimidation.

"Take the dress off your wife," he ordered. "Leave the lingerie and shoes."

Diane looked at me and smiled bravely as I stood before her and lifted the white dress over her head. Then, she was naked except for the uncharacteristic bra and panties. I hung the garment back in Diane's closet and watched as Deacon had her lay face down on the bed and spread her arms and legs.

"Attach her wrist and ankle on that side," he instructed. So, I did, placing the restraints on my wife's arms and legs and buckling them down tight. Quickly, she was spread eagle, on her stomach, with her face buried in a pillow, still clad in bra and panties.

That, however, did not last long.

From among the many implements and gadgets he had unpacked, Deacon brought out a knife, long, sharp. He held it like a man who knows how to hold a knife holds a knife. He moved it toward my wife's prone and helpless body and I gasped. Then, startled by my outburst, Diane awkwardly cranked her head around as much as she could considering her situation, and she also gasped and screamed.

"Shhh," he told us both. Then once we had quieted, he held the knife near Diane's back and inserting it between her skin and the lacy material, cut the back of the bra strap in one quick stroke. Then, in the same efficient manner, he severed both shoulder straps and they lay useless across her pale white back.

Diane struggled against the restraints and I watched, helplessly as Deacon then split her discreet, white panties up the back, exposing the perfect half-moons of her butt. He then placed the knife among the other implements of torture he had brought and picked up something comprised of a handle and multiple strands hanging from it. Like a leather mop. Deacon glanced my way and noted my confusion.

"This," he explained, "Is a flogger." He began twirling it in the air skillfully as he continued to speak. "And, this, is warm up." Then, having said that, he struck Dianes bare back lightly with the flogger. Then slightly harder, and I heard my wife moan. It wasn't a sound she made in pain, but one almost of relief as the man in black continued his assault, with increasing intensity until finally, she did emit a groan that told us both she was feeling something that crossed the border between pleasure and pain. It was at this point that he began to work on her buttocks and legs, then moving down, he struck the soles of her feet lightly, then more firmly. Finally, when the flogger had done its work on every part of the rear parts of her body, he stopped and spent several seconds admiring his handiwork.

"Undo the cuffs on your side," he commanded. I jumped to obey. Once her limbs were free, she lay inert and Deacon addressed me again.

"Let's flip her over," I was told, and together the two of us turned Diane so she was face-up on the bed, and hurriedly resecured, spread eagle. He looked at her contemplatively, stroking his chin and then running his palm over his smooth skull before going to his array of tools and coming back to her carrying something shiny. He then reached with his free hand and stroked her right breast, kneading and massaging, before taking her nipple and pinching it which caused her to gasp and arch her back up off the mattress. Then, he placed the shiny object that was in his other hand on the erect and swollen nipple, and Diane cried out. When Deacon stepped away, I saw he had placed on her a wicked-looking clamp, retreated to the treasure trove, and brought back another so that the left breast would not feel neglected after giving it the same attention as the right, he applied the painful implement. She cried out and thrashed and pulled on the cuffs until finally, he dropped his hands down between her legs. As he stroked her pussy lips she started to squirm and make sounds that were almost otherworldly. They were testimonies to the pleasure he was causing her to feel. Then, as he continued, the tone changed. Pain was being introduced, subtly at first, then more overtly, until she was crying out in a combination of anguish and desire. It was at that point, that he went back to the toy pile and came back with other shiny objects. When he applied them to her cunt, I heard my wife scream, then groan and shake the bed. It was like watching a real-life scene from *The Exorcist*, as she shrieked and cursed. Meanwhile, Deacon began stroking her, and then placing fingers inside her dripping hole, until the cries of pain turned to cries of pleasure. Then once she began emitting a steady stream of mewling and cooing , Deacon went back to the toys and came back with a new instrument of torture. Another flogger, this one with tendrils of rubber, and when he struck her the first time, on her flat, toned belly, made a sickening thudding sound, even though the blow was delivered with no intensity and that point. The next was slightly harder, then he moved to her legs, assiduously avoiding her clamped pussy, going down her exposed and vulnerable thighs and feet. Then back up those same areas, until he had Diane purring like a happy kitty.

Then the targets of his assault changed. At which point, she rapidly went from happy kitty to angry alley cat. He began directing the flogger to strike the clamps holding her nipples, both breasts, which caused shrieks of pain. Then, he aimed at her entrapped pussy lips and the deafening expressions of outrage and the resultant writhing in agony as Diane's naked, bound body danced to the tune being played by her new Bull.

Finally, his blows slowed, and grew less intense, until he was lightly stroking her inflamed flesh. Then, after placing the rubber flogger alongside his other tools, he gently took the clamps from each affected body part, the removal of which caused a gasp and a pained cry, and then as he massaged the blood back into them, different sounds. Sounds of pleasure. His tender ministrations had my wife humming pleasantly as he backed away from her and undid his belt, a move that caused Diane to crook her neck toward him and smile. He kicked off his heavy boots and lowered his jeans and then his briefs, stepping out of them and moving toward where Diane lay bound and waiting. In two steps, his long, thick cock was bobbing before her eyes, as he climbed on the bed and straddled her prone body. He sat across her sore breasts and dangled his hard cock in front of her hungry mouth.

"Suck me," he told her, but even before his command, she was straining toward his engorged member, finally trapping it between her lips and beginning her happy task. Soon she was making slurping sounds as he pushed his hips forward and actively fucked her throat. Finally, he withdrew, and as she gasped for air, Deacon scooted down Diane's body until he was between her spread legs and had the tip of his cock, slick with her saliva, poised at the entrance to her sore but ready cunt.

He drove in swiftly and mercilessly, going balls deep in one stroke, then grinding into her until she groaned in both agony and ecstasy. She swore and also called to her creator as he began a piston-like pounding that shook her body and the bed, a violent rhythm that caused me to shudder and at the same time excited me to the point that my cockhead peeked out of my skirt. I reached to tuck back in but instead began to stroke myself until I saw Deacon looking at what I was doing. I hesitated a second until he nodded and then I worked myself faster and harder, my stroking almost in time with his fucking my wife. Then, as if we had planned it, the three of us all cried out in mutual orgasms. Diane was shaking and crying out loudly as my seed spilled onto the bedroom carpet and the Bull shot into my wife.

WE ALL COLLAPSED. ME AGAINST THE wall, Diane on the bed, and Deacon on my wife. We lay inert a long time, but Deacon stirred first, uncuffing Diane without my help and embracing her warmly and kissing her lightly and without the passion of earlier in the evening.

"Well, how was it?" He asked while still laying on her. The question coaxed what I interpreted as a thoughtful look on her face.

"I liked it," was her answer as he climbed off her and pulled his pants on, then his boots.

"You'll be sore in the morning," he warned. "Best to take something for the pain." Then he pointed at me. "You might want to have your maid get you a drink to go with it. Something stronger than white wine."

The memory made her wince.

"Drinking that sweet shit was more painful than the floggers," she commented wryly.

Deacon packed his things neatly back into the satchel and was soon ready to depart. He leaned over and kissed Diane gently on the lips and she kissed him back, also gently without the need she had before.

"Call me," he told her.

"Definitely," she said in response, "We are on for next week, right?"

"Yes, we are," he confirmed. "You gonna get the clothes we talked about?"

Diane giggled, and replied, "Yes." The giggle worried me but the worry was forgotten as the man once again in black, put his fingers to his lips and kissed them and waved goodbye to the beautiful blonde woman on the bed who not too long before had been his willing "victim."

I led him to the door in silence. Once we were in the portico there was an awkward pause on my part. I had a question I felt funny asking, but my curiosity couldn't keep me from it.

"I dressed like this for tonight," I began and fidgeted and smoothed my skirt and adjusted my bra as I carefully approached the subject.

"Yes." he replied blandly, "Yes you did."

"Well," I tried to stammer out what I meant to ask, "Will I be expected to dress like this every time you visit?"

Deacon looked at me and laughed.

"You'll have to ask your wife about that," he said as he pulled open the door, "The maid's outfit was her idea. To tell you the truth, she's wrong. You do have the legs to pull it off."

# 13

"Yes," my wife said as we sat together watching TV. "Yes, mom. So exciting. Yes, mom." Finally, Diane looked at me and after making that motion people make with their hands to indicate someone won't shut up, she held her glass toward me. The international distress signal indicating alcohol deprivation. Taking the hint, I took her glass, and went down the well-worn path to our bar, to crack another obscenely expensive bottle of Johnny Walker Blue. There were many needs my wife had that I could not satisfy. Scotch was not among those, so doing what I was capable , I mixed her cocktail and took it to her. She was still on the phone with her mother, and as I approached, she put her hand to her throat which seemed to indicate either desperate thirst or that if she would strangle herself.

It seemed to be both as Diane took a long sip, said, "Yes mom," one more time then, "Love you mom" and "Bye mom," and pressed the end call button, releasing her from her long cellular ordeal.

"That was mom," she said as she put her glass on the coffee table and wiped a few drops of scotch and soda off her lips. After she said that I gasped audibly and tried to make a face indicating amazement. Diane laughed. I always had the ability to make Diane laugh. Sometimes it was even intentional. She took another sip and continued speaking.

"Guess what," she began. "Dana's pregnant."

I did another gasp, this time louder and more theatrical, and simultaneously placed a hand on either side of my face in an expression of shock. Diane laughed so hard she almost spilled her scotch.

"Yes, I was amazed too." She placed her glass down again, only to pick it back up for another sip. "Seriously though, Dana asked me to not tell Mom I knew before her. At least I respect her wishes, even if she doesn't always respect mine."

I nodded and she continued.

"She's obviously excited," my wife told me. "It's her first grandchild. Her telling me led to the inevitable guilting that I never had kids."

"Did you tell her you'd rather eat bagels?" I asked.

"Toasted," she reminded me. "With cream cheese. No, I didn't. I don't think she would have seen that as a reasonable defense, so I threw myself on the mercy of the court and listened."

"That law school training comes in handy, doesn't it?" I took a sip of my own drink after I said it. Diane nodded and shifted to try to find a comfortable position in which to sit. That had become an issue after Deacon's visit two nights earlier. The first night she had slept on ice packs. The soreness and bruising had slowly begun to recede but not completely. However, when I asked if it had been worth the resultant pain, my wife replied definitely. Then while she was thinking, she informed me the sadistic bull wasn't scheduled for a return engagement until the following week.

"Why so long Puddin?" I asked as she tried in vain to find a way to position her body that did not make it ache. She looked at me and scowled.

"Eugene will be here Friday, right?" She asked, ignoring my sarcasm. I responded with a nod. "And Donald?" I answered with another nod.

"Saturday," I replied.

"No Tim?" She took the controller and started to channel surf, apparently liking my program selection about as much as she liked my dick.

This time I shook my head. "He has a convention this week."

"A pet food convention?" she said, finally settling on a cooking show.

"Must be," I replied.

"I wonder what they do at pet food conventions?" she asked as she clicked off the cooking show and onto other things which interested her more than cooking. Like anything in the world.

"Hmm," I responded contemplatively. "Maybe chew on each other's kibbles and bits?"

Diane exploded into a huge guffaw, which ended quickly when she realized it aggravated her soreness. She looked at me and smiled and shook her head. It was those looks that got me through what had become a life of endless debauchery for her and endless humiliations for me. Those looks told me, she fucked them, but she loved me.

Finally, she settled on a movie that we had both seen several times. That way we could ignore it and continue to talk.

"So," I began, as a car chase ended in a fiery crash on screen. "Mom's excited?"

"Oh God, yes," Diane replied watching as a Corvette burned to the frame. "While we were talking, she was shopping for baby clothes online."

I winced as the explosion of the Corvette's gas tank shook the room thanks to the miracle of surround sound.

"Maybe they will name the baby Sean Junior," I joked after recovering my faculties. Diane laughed again because everybody loves a funny cuck.

"Actually, if it's a boy she wants Dana to name it for her father," she replied.

"Not for your father?" I thought I knew the answer before I asked but didn't know what else to say.

"Mom hated our father," my wife noted confirming what I already knew to be true. Diane and Dana's parents had been married for over 50 tumultuous years, during which time their father had tried to dominate the women in his life until Diane eventually rebelled and escaped. He'd died the year before his daughter and I met. Often, I wondered if the fact that I sought to maintain marital harmony at any cost was what kept her with me. That and the fact if we split, she would be condemned to an endless stream of take-out food and TV dinners which she would eat watching cooking shows she didn't understand. Besides, who else would make her laugh as I could?

THE FACT THAT I WAS ALSO NOW SCHEDULING HER "play dates" was another quality I was sure she found endearing. That advantage of remaining my lawfully wedded wife manifested itself the next Friday when Eugene appeared at our door carrying a bottle of wine and a dozen roses. Though I answered the door not dressed as "Jacqueleen" I knew my purpose was the same. Help facilitate the night's festivities.

I escorted the ebony giant to the master bedroom, though he knew the way by then. Diane was waiting for him, lying on our bed, naked. Apparently, that night she had decided to hasten the process by cutting out steps, one of which was undressing. Eugene stopped in the doorway and looked appreciatively at my wife.

"What a lovely prelude to dinner," he said to her. "A delicious appetizer."

She smiled and spread out more fully.

"Just consider me your whore d'oeuvre," she remarked. as he dropped his pants and descended upon her. Once they were fully engaged sexually, I went back to the kitchen to finish dinner prep, that having become the expected routine when Eugene visited. Tonight, was leg of lamb night, with carrots and scallions and new potatoes. Eugene had two portions of everything, including the key lime pie I had made for dessert. He then adjourned to the bedroom for seconds of my wife.

"Undress Diane, while I watch," he ordered as he sat on the edge of my bed. The process was simple and quick, since, after their initial coupling, she had put on a simple yellow sundress and no underwear. Once I lifted the loose garment off her, she stood gloriously naked except for her high-heeled shoes, which coordinated perfectly with what she had been wearing, but also looked damn good with what she had on then, which was nothing.

"Now undress me," Eugene told me. This was a more complicated process, as he had gotten completely redressed for dinner, including his necktie, which was the first thing I removed, undoing the Windsor knot, and draping it on the same hanger on which I placed his shirt after I unbuttoned and took it off him. Then his shoes, pants, and underwear, and he stood before us tall, proud, and completely nude. A Masai warrior whose "spear" was at full mast and ready to attack.

"Now you undress, Jack." He said it matter of factly, but the implications always made me shiver nervously. The obvious comparisons that would not flatter me. The humiliation of my wife's scorn was truly cutting.

Naturally, I was rock hard, a fact that was glaringly obvious once I had dropped my pants and briefs. Also, a fact glaringly ignored by Diane as she eagerly anticipated a second helping of "dark meat." First Eugene had another command. He directed her to lay splay legged leaning against the pillows stacked against the headboard of our bed. Then he pointed to my wife's glistening pussy.

"Get her ready," he ordered.

I looked at him, then at her sex, then back at him, and he nodded. So, I crawled tentatively up on the bed, between her outstretched legs. As I got closer, the more apparent evidence of the big man's previous use became. Her cunt gleamed with the juices her excitement was producing. There were also dried patches of sticky whiteness where he had cum and it had dried on her pale pink lips. My head dipped to go to her used and battered slit, but before I did, I looked back at Eugene, who nodded again, and I heard Diane giggle above me and so I pressed my face to her pussy and kissed then licked, then delved, then probed. It's a misconception that after as long a period of time as it had taken us to eat dinner that there were wells of semen left for the cuck to lick. The body's processes eliminate that, But, there is a residual "taste" leftover that mingles with the woman's natural flavors that indicate another man had been there. Most of what leads to many men's abhorrence is mental. The very idea that another man's semen had been there and would be again. The idea that this was now the bull's "territory" and the cuck had been given a conditional pass, and he best tread carefully. As I worked her folds with my tongue, my wife began to moan then writhe then shake, and finally, I felt a big finger, tapping me on the shoulder. It broke my concentration and I turned my head to see Eugene standing waiting.

"My turn," he said smiling. So, I scooted out of his way and got off the bed and went to my chair, and sat, watching as his thick, veiny member disappeared into my wife's well licked pussy, after which he began a strong, steady pounding that had her groaning, then gasping, then screaming in the throes of orgasm. Once she had been sated, and only after, the big man roared like an African lion as he came inside her once again.

Then he slowed to a halt like a powerful freight train and lay on her a while in recovery. Finally, he pushed himself up and looked at me, and grinned.

"Do we have any of that pie left, Jack?" He asked. I assured him we did, and if we didn't, I'd have baked him another out of respect for a superb performance. He nimbly raised himself to a sitting position on the edge of the bed and grabbed his slacks. As we were redressing Diane spoke without looking up.

"You boys go get some pie," she said weakly. "I'm stuffed."

Eugene put on his dress shirt and draped his tie around his neck, then reached down and gently patted my wife's thigh.

"Yes," he said. "Yes, you were." Then we headed to the kitchen for the necessary post-coital sustenance.

# 14

Bradley's battered truck rolled in and parked in the drive around 9 Saturday night. He wasted no time vaulting through the door and down the hall and almost as soon as he had entered my bedroom, he had entered my wife, pummeling her pussy while simultaneously gnawing her breasts and nipples as she savagely clawed his back. The intensity of their coupling seemed more urgent than usual, and almost before I had settled into my chair, the show was over, and Donald was pulling up his black slacks and departing in the same swift manner he had arrived, leaving me disappointed, but my wife sexually satisfied. Which was really what this was all about. I guess.

"He was on his break," Diane said, responding to a question I hadn't asked. "He told me when he came in, he didn't have much time."

"Seems like he made the most of it," I replied. Diane smiled.

"Me. Too," she said happily. Then a message chimed in on her phone.

"Bradley," she explained. "He has a few minutes left and wanted to thank me."

"As well he should," I told her.

"True," she replied laughing, "after all how many women would give a guy a 'flying fuck?'"

"Hmmm," she said looking at her phone, "Bradley just told me he met Dana."

"Met?" I asked.

"Met as in had sex with," she explained with a look on her face that seemed a mix of anger and amazement.

"NO!" I exclaimed!

"Here," she said turning the phone so I could see the screen.

Diane; *You fucked.*
Bradley: *We fucked.*
Diane: *WTF????*

The message went on to say Bradley was going off break and would explain later.

"Later" turned out to be 3:27 a.m. and Diane and I were dozing on the couch.

"You're kidding," Diane exclaimed into the phone. Once again, she had in her earbuds and I could only hear her side of the conversation.

"You're kidding," she said again, and then altered it to "You are kidding." Then, "I don't believe it," and finally (again), "You're kidding," after which she said goodbye and pulling her earbuds out of her ears shut off the phone. I waited expectantly as she placed her phone on the cocktail table.

"So?" I said finally, as she settled back on the couch. "Dana is cheating on Dan with one of his waiters?" The realization struck me that most of the networks had dropped soap operas, and they were all now being played out by my wife and her family.

Diane shook her head and smiled. Not a happy smile, but a smile, nonetheless.

"No," she told me. "She's not cheating on Dan. Dan set it up."

"You're kidding," I didn't have to fake my amazement. This time I was legitimately stunned.

"Yup," my wife answered, "Donald said Dan arranged for him to meet Dana."

"But he had to know what would happen," I replied. "No offense to your sister but . . ." I let the sentence dangle.

"No offense taken," Diane replied. "She's a slut. We all know that. Except for maybe Mom. She thinks Dana's the 'good girl' and I'm the slut."

I shook my head.

"So, what do you think Dan's up to now? He set up the woman who's carrying his child to have sex with another man."

"Bingo," she said pointing a meticulously manicured finger at me. I knew the manicure job was meticulous because I had done it the day before so she would look good for the weekend. Which is why when she was clawing Donald's back, I wanted to say to her, "Honey, don't chip the polish."

Diane stretched, yawned, and struggled to get up off the couch. I stood at the same time and when I did, she reached out her hand and I pulled her to her feet, and arm in arm, we headed to the bedroom.

"Jackie," she asked sleepily, "am I a slut?"

We walked slowly down the hall together as I thought about it.

"Yes," I replied, then added, "but you are an ethical slut."

She hugged me and put her head on my shoulder.

"Good answer," she said. "Oh, just wait till Deacon's here the next time. We are going to have such fun."

I turned back the covers and we got in bed. She was still holding me and she dozed off quickly. On the other hand, I lay there replaying what my wife had just said. The fear and excitement kept me awake until almost dawn.

## 15

"Your cummerbund is hanging in the closet along with your tie." Diane was hustling around our bedroom wearing frilly white lingerie and stockings, not long after having gotten back from having her hair professionally done. It wasn't cheap, but I had to admit it was a work of art. She'd had her makeup done there, and it was gorgeous. Better than I could have done, and I'd gotten pretty good. Did it say something about the priorities of a cuckold that I fixated more on my wife's makeup job and how I could duplicate it, than how her bountiful breasts were spilling out of her lacy bra? I decided it did and I also decided that I needed to use more eye shadow next time. I also decided that I was happy dressing in male clothes rather than as Jacqueleen the French maid. After all, Deacon was coming. I was only in my tux shirt. I needed to get dressed before my wife changed her mind. I quickly stepped into my tux pants, feeling fortunate that for now she was distracted, having disappeared into her own closet. That was a place I almost never ventured since it looked like Dresden after several bombing raids. Today I had not been allowed in, saying her new outfit was a "surprise" for me. Though by then I considered myself surprise proof, I had to admit to feeling no little shock when Diane stepped back into the bedroom in a long, white wedding dress.

"Do you like it?" She asked, looking at me, smiling that smile she had that dared me to guess what was next.

"You look stunning," was all I could say.

"You look stunned," she replied laughing as she looked in the mirror and straightened her lacey and low-cut bodice. "Finish getting dressed, then you can help me with my train."

Hooking up my cummerbund, I then fastened my ready-tied bowtie around my shirt collar. Once those were in place I hustled over to where Diane was still primping and awaited directions. She had not dressed in anything nearly so elaborate when we had gotten married. A simple off-white dress and a bouquet had sufficed for standing before a judge who was a personal friend of hers. I wore one of my blue suits. The service was quick and we were drinking at the bar at the airport awaiting a flight to Maui in short order. This was different. If this was a renewal of our vows, I wondered if my wife would have me re-up the vow of chastity, I seemed to have taken the last several months. How long did I have to go without sex to be eligible to wear virginal white?

We had just gotten Diane's wedding trousseau all assembled when the doorbell rang.

"Deacons here," my wife said, her voice a mixture of anticipation and dread. "Get the door."

As I went to do as ordered, I did so with less anticipation than dread. My dread grew exponentially when I saw that Deacon was dressed like a priest. My reaction amused him. Stunned had become my "go-to" look.

"Bless you, my son," he said as he came in carrying his black leather satchel. Twelve years of Catholic school caused me to respond reflexively as I replied, "Thank you, Father."

"Dearly beloved," Deacon said as we stood before him in our living room. As he read off the words, we were side by side. The furniture had been pushed to the side and we had plenty of space for the "ceremony." Something told me this would not very closely resemble our first nuptials, except for the part where we drank afterward. In fact, at that moment, I felt as if I needed one. Especially when he came to the part where he asked, "Diane, do you take Jack to be your lawfully wedded husband?" To which my wife responded by smiling, looking at me, and almost surprisingly saying "Yes." Then the kicker as she said to Father Deacon," But, I'd rather take you first." Then, having stated that desire, she handed me her bouquet, dropped to her knees like a sorrowful penitent, and attacked the hassock of his priestly robes, quickly drawing out his already hardened cock, and immediately took it between her lips and began to suck hungrily. As I stood holding the flowers my wife had given me, Deacon threw back his head as the bride played a recital on his organ. He was so caught up in receiving pleasure he dropped the bible he'd held, and they both were so involved in their illicit act that they ignored the loud thump the book made when it hit the floor. I didn't ignore it. The harsh sound made me jump. Or maybe I was just tense because my wedding ceremony had been interrupted by oral sex between my wife and the officiant.

When he finally could no longer hold up under Diane's expert ministrations, he took her by the hands, and had her lie on the carpet, as I stepped out of their way so as not to be crushed in their rush to consummate my marriage. He ripped off the lacy white panties she had worn apparently so he could do just what he did. After her pussy was bared, he entered her and they fucked with wild abandon. No matter how often I saw my wife have sex with other men, the sight never ceased to fascinate me and my reaction even more so. Watching excited me and my own cock grew hard from the combination of shame and frustration. Putting the bouquet in my left hand, I unzipped my tux pants and withdrew my stiffened member, and began to work it, in time with Deacon's thrusts, until finally, we all three orgasmed as one and a priest on my wife in my living room and I looked down and saw the semen stains I had left on our living room rug.

True to my expectation, afterward, when Diane had cleaned up and Deacon and I had zipped up, we sat in the living room and had drinks. He had helped me push the furniture back to its normal placement. Once two rounds had been imbibed, Deacon made his exit, leaving the bride and groom alone once again.

"Well," Diane said as she held her glass toward me in a display of her unspoken need. "Were you shocked?"

I took the glass and stood. Then I bent and kissed my wife on the lips. Lips that had not long before been wrapped around the cock of another man. She kissed me back, with a warmth that always heartened me and encouraged me to go on.

"Diane," I said before heading to the bar. "After all, we have been through together, I think I am well beyond shock. I will say this, after tonight, I am certain we are both going to hell."

Diane grinned at me broadly.

"Yeah," she replied. "You're probably right, but you have to admit, we are having a lot of fun getting there."

## 16

"Do you see? I really am starting to show."

My sister-in-law was visiting and I was serving her and my wife lunch. The pair were eating chicken salad sandwiches and discussing Dana's pregnancy.

"Has the morning sickness been bad?" Diane asked after chewing and swallowing a bite of her sandwich. Dana nodded in vigorous affirmation.

"Girl, it's been a puke fest," Dana replied to which Diane responded by making a face that indicated she was neither anxious to experience such a thing, nor did she want to discuss it over lunch Dana, oblivious to others as always, continued to describe in vivid detail her trials and tribulations since having a bun placed in her oven. Finally, having had enough talk of regurgitation, my wife decided to change the subject to a topic she much preferred.

"So, how is pregnancy sex?" She asked as I cleared her plate away. I then gathered Danas and mine and hurried them to the kitchen, so as to avoid being a witness to an awkward discussion of her various liaisons with men who were not her husband, or an impediment that would prevent Diane from getting the information she sought. Her law school training had kicked in and whether Dana knew it or not, she was about to undergo a cross-examination.

"CALL MOM," DANA SAID AS SHE WAS KISSING her sister's cheek before she left two hours later. Diane assured her she would. Then Dana headed to the door, but only after she gave me a contemptuous look that made me cringe. I managed a weak smile, as she exited the house. Once she had closed the door, my wife crossed her arms in front of her chest, a move that lifted her firm full breasts seductively. The view distracted me 'till Diane roused me back to attention.

"Jack," She snapped. Then she pointed two fingers at her face, "Eyes, up here." I lifted my head and looked at her in response.

"Sorry dear," I said sheepishly. Diane shook her head.

"Men," she declared as if that's all that needed to be said, then headed to the living room.

"Do we have any beer?" She asked. I responded in the affirmative. By beer, she meant the new hard seltzers that I had begun to buy for her that she'd taken a liking to. I opened one for her and we headed to the back yard and we sat together on the glider, a place where the memories of seeing my wife openly fellate her then lover and bull had begun to fade. Replaced by newer, fresher, more disturbing mental images.

It was spring, and the weather was getting warmer and the flowers had begun to emerge. We sat and for a long time didn't feel the need to talk.

"How's Bradley?" I asked finally, never at a loss for the wrong question. Diane snorted in response.

"He will never be Dan to Dana," she said between sips of seltzer.

"Maybe that's a good thing," I replied taking a sip of my own. The sip made me wonder why I was drinking it. I didn't like it and we had real beer in the fridge. I had grabbed it when I grabbed hers and was committed to finish what I started like all other aspects of my life. It occurred to me that my marriage was living proof of that.

That thought made me think about it further, but another sip and ingesting more alcohol would solve that.

"No guy will ever be Dan to me," Diane said thoughtfully leaning back and letting the afternoon sunshine on her face. "And, that my darling, is a very good thing."

We sat together and sipped and didn't talk again for a while. I'd known Diane for over four years by then and could read her moods. As quiet as she seemed at that moment, she was restless. Eugene was out of town with his wife and hadn't visited Friday and Diane had seemed less interested in Bradley since she found out he was fucking her sister and the others, she seemed to have less interest in lately. I knew my wife, and my wife was bored. Restless and bored. As nervous as it made me, I had an idea, that I'd had for a while, but was afraid to bring up. It could be exciting, but also, be fraught with peril. In other words, right up Diane's alley. What the hell, I thought, In for a penny, in for a pound and I took her empty can and mine in my one hand and took her by the hand and drug her off the glider with the other.

"C'mon, darling." I said as she stood looking at me curiously, "Get cleaned up and changed. We are going out clubbing."

# 17

By 7:45 Diane was showered and coiffed and made up and having dressed three different times she and I were meeting our Uber in front of the house. I had thought about driving, but considering the events I had set in motion, I felt it would be better if I could drink. So, I opened the door of a midnight blue Acura and Diane got in, then, getting in myself, we set out on another adventure.

The club we had decided on was just far enough off downtown to give it an edgy feel. The strobe lights were strobing and the music blaring and I felt a twinge in my belly from being a "man out of time." I fit in like a skunk at a butterfly convention, not only age-wise, but also in racial terms. While several of the women in attendance were white, I was the only Caucasian male in the place. Not that it seemed to attract the attention of the clubbers. They were concentrating on my wife. I was merely there to pay the tab and hold her purse when she went to the lady's room. Everyone else, both male and female, were focused on the woman at my side. Stunningly beautiful and dressed in a style that was just barely street-legal. Her bright red dress was low but enough in front to display the gorgeous breasts I had ogled earlier in the day and was also so short that if she bent at all some ass cheek peeked out. Adding to the excitement of that for herself, me, and those around us was she had not put on any panties. Matching six-inch heels completed the ensemble and as she strutted in, every eye was on her. Especially the male eyes, but even a few of the female eyes. Watching them watch her made me wonder, was it envy, or lust? There was no doubt as to the source of the men's attention. They fairly burned with desire. I was largely ignored, a fact that made me grateful.

I fought for space at the bar, trying to cut through the assembled masses to get us our drinks. After a few fruitless attempts on my part, my wife took the lead and the barflies parted like the Red Sea as I was pushed farther and farther away from her. We had a purpose for going there, but unless I took action, this was going to be out of control quickly. Luckily enough, I saw my refuge and went toward it. There was a small high-top table not far off the dance floor that had been recently vacated. Grabbing. Diane's hand I dove on it as quickly as dragging her in her ridiculous shoes would allow. As littered as it was with empty glasses and soiled cocktail napkins, it was a place to sit that was not the bar. Now the prospects could come to us and my wife could sort through them without it being a mob scene. I was getting the hang of this cuckolding thing, a fact that both made me proud and vaguely disturbed me.

The first man who approached was tall and slim. Not thin, but lean, with an obvious musculature under his trendy suit. He brought her another drink even though she had barely taken two sips out of the one she already had in front of her. She took what appeared to be a fruity concoction and thanked the man without asking his name. He understood the snub and stomped away huffily. Once he was gone, I reached for the drink and sniffed it.

"Don't drink that," Diane warned. I looked at her quizzically.

"There's something in it," she explained. "Ever heard of roofies?"

I placed the glass back on the table carefully and looked at it like it was about to explode. By the time I looked up, my wife's attention had moved on to surveying the bar for other men whose intentions were not drug-induced rape.

Then at almost the same moment, we spied someone. Tall and strong looking, in a tight black t-shirt, his skin was the color of caramel. The hair on his head was closely cropped and neat, as was the hair on his face. He looked toward our table and I saw his eyes lock on Diane. She noticed it too and tried to look away and failed. His dark eyes and chiseled features were an obvious source of fascination and finally, he made his way to her.

"Good evening," he said, in an accent, I took to be African. Maybe Kenyan? "I'm Bronson, and you two are . . . ?"

My wife smiled broadly.

"I'm Diane," she said in a breathy voice, "and he is leaving so you can sit down." She waved her hand at me in a gesture I took to mean, "Shoo." Taking the hint, I got up from my chair so my wife's new "friend" could take my place. Recent experience told me that wasn't going to be the last time that night he would replace me.

"I do need to use the men's room," I told them. "Here," I said to Bronson, "You can keep her company." He smiled and made a deferential gesture but did not defer to the extent of declining my offer.

"Are you sure?" He asked with no sincerity at all.

"Be my guest," I replied. "I have bladder problems so I may be gone a while."

I was certain he had not heard what I'd said as his focus was, by then, fully on my wife. I then stepped away to perform one of the duties of a cuckold husband. To watch and wait.

It only took finishing her first drink to get Diane and Bronson on the dance floor. They danced well together, moving in a coordinated fluid grace. They weren't Fred and Ginger, but the ways they flowed in unison made me speculate as to how they would mesh later that night. This not being my first rodeo, I could see how things were trending. Something told me that at the end of the night, Diane and Bronson would be together in my bed and I would be sitting alone in my chair watching.

As it turned out I got some things wrong. They ended up in his bed, in a trendy downtown loft a short drive from the club. So as a result, I was not in my chair, opting instead to lean on one of the stylish brick walls that formed Bronson's apartment. Another assumption I'd had that was wrong was that I would be watching them alone. I was not alone. Three of Bronson's friends had accompanied us back to the loft, and stood against the wall with me, watching like me. Unlike me, however, they were obviously waiting their turn, as their friend's lithe body moved smoothly over my wife's pale flesh. The contrast was striking. Both beautiful and arousing as he pleasured and pleased her with his ample endowment. His cock was long and thin with a large bulbous head that, judging from Diane's reactions hit all the right spots. Finally, after several sessions of writhing, grinding, mewling, and screaming, she was done with him and he climbed off, opening space for one of the men with whom I'd been waiting and watching. He was black like Bronson, but his skin was a darker shade, more mahogany, than oak, with a short-cropped hairstyle and a cock that was, like him, short and thick. Once he was fully naked, she beckoned him to her head and took him in her mouth, gently, as though the hunger within her had been sated and she was now doing what she was doing out of pleasure rather than need. Watching her reminded me of two things. One was that she had savage and ravenous appetites, and the second thing was that I could never satisfy them myself. It's why I was doing what I did.

As the new couple performed Bronson took a place on the wall beside me and watched. He had not redressed, apparently in anticipation of subsequent "bites of the apple." As his friend knelt between my wife's spread legs, Bronson's cock began to find a new lease on life. He didn't touch it. I on the other hand began rubbing my stiffening member through my slacks and briefs until finally, I became aware of the fact that Bronson was looking at me. I took notice at the exact moment Diane cried out in orgasmic delight and that got both our attentions on the carnal activities on the bed, next to which the other two men were casually stripping out of their clothes in preparation. As Shakespeare once wrote, "Readiness is all." It was at that point that, without losing focus on his friend dismounting the beautiful blonde in his bed, Bronson spoke.

"You should go home, my friend."

He said it matter of factly, but I was stunned.

"No," I replied weakly. "She needs me to stay." Bronson shook his head.

"This could take a while," he replied mildly. "I will take care of her and bring her to you when we are done."

This time I shook my head, but like the no, it was a weak protestation. Meanwhile, Diane was between paramours, had noticed what was going on, and crooked her finger at me. I got off the wall and knelt beside the bed. She looked at me and smiled sweetly, lovingly, and placed her palm on my cheek gently. Her other hand took mine and held it tightly. Then, she said in a soft, tender, yet firm voice:

"Go home, Jack."

So, very few minutes later I was on the street in front of Bronson's building waiting on an Uber, which turned out to be a silver Honda driven by a swarthy middle-aged man named Ahmed. He took me home quickly and efficiently and dropped me off to endure what I had become accustomed to but still had not gotten used to. The long, lonely night of the cuck.

# 18

It was late Sunday evening when I finally heard Diane's key in our front door. I was watching a movie on Netflix, which I paused when she entered. Unlike her previous foray into group sex, she did not look like she'd been ravaged by a pack of hungry wolverines. In fact, she looked none the worse for wear. Physically tired but with a brightness in her eyes that told me our night out had accomplished its purpose.

"Hi," she said as she crossed to where I was sitting and kissed me on the head. Looking up at her I smiled to the greatest extent that was possible given the situation. I was bothered. Not at what had happened. I had set the whole thing into motion. I was glad she was once more, happy and satisfied. That wasn't why I was bothered. What bothered me was that I wanted details. I needed to feed the perverse excitement our new arrangement had engendered within me. Diane noticed my annoyance, cocked her head, and looked back at me.

"What?" She asked simply, though I knew she understood what was happening. She was testing me. The law school training had kicked in and she wanted a confession. Looking at her sourly, I finally relented and gave her what she sought.

"What happened?" I asked in exasperation. She laughed and turned toward the bedroom.

"Come on then," she said in a more than condescending tone. "I'll tell you while we get ready for bed. Unless you want to stay up and finish your movie."

I powered down the flatscreen and got off the couch. Real life had become more dramatic than any show on TV, streaming, or cable, and if I couldn't be one of the actors, or even be in the audience, I wanted to hear all about it.

Once we were in our bedroom, Diane sat on the edge of the bed and kicked off her shoes. She pushed her bare right foot toward me and I reflexively knelt before her and began to rub her tired and tender toes.

"Oooh," she cooed, "That feels like heaven honey. Not as good as those young cocks that filled me all night . . . all day too. But it feels good." I worked on the right foot a while then, finally, she replaced it with the left, which I massaged as she lay back on the bed and described in excruciating detail the wonders she had experienced in Bronson's loft.

"Oh God, honey," she exclaimed, "their cocks were so good." Her voice had the smooth sweet quality of honey when she said it. My own dick was as stiff as it could possibly get as I massaged her feet and listened. This was in spite of how many times I had masturbated thinking of what was happening since leaving Bronson's place and the orgy taking place within it, with my wife as the mistress of ceremonies. As she enthused over her most recent liaison she reached and peeled her dress off over her head and tossed it aside, knowing I would pick it up later. She was naked underneath as she usually was when she returned from such activities, the expensive lingerie discarded somewhere in Bronson's flat. The garments were gone, but the credit card bills lingered on.

Reaching up, she began massaging her breasts and tweaking her nipples as I continued my careful ministrations to her feet. As she stimulated herself, she began to moan and the activity and the sound combined with the fragrant scent of her pussy drew my attention up her body until finally, my gaze came to rest on her pussy. There, above her cleft, in the bare region that for years been the forest of pubic hair she never felt the need to groom for me, was something new, and seeing it startled and disturbed me. It was a tattoo. A dark mark. A symbol I recognized from a playing card. It was a spade, and as I stared at it, I realized it had a capital Q in the middle. I had never seen such a mark in real life, but I could guess the significance, and the realization stunned and aroused me.

Diane noticed me staring and it made her giggle. She took her hands off her breasts and placed one hand on my head like you would pat a puppy while the other went to her newly decorated mons.

"Like it?" She asked coyly. "It was Bronson's idea." I was speechless. All I could do was nod and continue to stare. My fascination made her giggle again and take my head in both her hands and pull me to her mound. I knew from experience what to do and began licking, which caused her giggles to turn to purrs.

"Mmmm," she said in a breathy voice, "that's it. Soothe my pussy. They bruised it so good. They pounded it, and now it's your turn. Pleasure your Queen of spades."

I DID JUST THAT, THREE TIMES IN FACT after which we climbed under the covers and held each other. She went to sleep immediately. It took me a while but finally, I drifted off. Later that morning, after a few hours of fitful sleep, I was awakened by the sound of the shower going in our bath and an empty space beside me in bed. Diane was already up and running. As I lay there trying to shake off the last revelations of Diane's early morning return, the shower sound stopped and my wife came into the bedroom, drying her tantalizingly damp body with a fluffy towel.

"Good morning sleepyhead," She said more cheerily than someone who'd had three hours sleep in two nights should say anything.

"Morning," I mumbled back, as I tried to, once again, bury my face in my pillow. Diane was having none of that, coming over to where I lay, carelessly tossing her towel on the floor so I would have something to pick up later. She shook me and demanded coffee until I reluctantly rolled over to comply. She was standing beside the bed stark naked, hands on her hips, shaking her head, and smiling. My eyes fought to focus. When they finally did, I noticed something. Her bare pussy was once again bare. No spade. No Q. Just smooth beautiful flesh. She noticed me noticing as she had earlier in the a.m., and it made her laugh. Not a giggle of amusement, but a satisfied chuckle.

"Wha . . ." I asked without finishing the word.

"It was a temporary tattoo, silly," She explained as though I were a child and a dull child at that. "Now get your ass out of bed and make me coffee. I need to get dressed. I have an early meeting."

Which I did, as well as toasting a raisin bagel and applying the usual generous portion of cream cheese. Once Diane came into the kitchen, she was dressed in her "lawyers' clothes," which that morning were a heather grey skirt suit over a periwinkle blue blouse, buttoned to a discreet lever, revealing almost no cleavage. Not none, but almost none. We sat together and drank our coffee and she ate her bagel with relish.

"Yum," she declared, "This is so decadent. I had so much exercise this weekend I needed the calories." When she said it, she looked at me and grinned. I smiled back, genuinely enjoying the fact that she was happy and fulfilled and that I had a hand in making it so. As she ate, she went on to explain the temporary tattoo.

"Bronson keeps a few handy, I guess," she told me. "He gets them off Amazon."

She bit off another bite of bagel and chewed.

"He put it on me before he brought me home," she said after she swallowed. "He said you'd freak out."

Looking at me she crooked an eyebrow.

"You didn't freak out too badly, though. Why is that?" She asked.

"Let's just say, I've come to expect the unexpected," I replied after taking a sip of my own coffee.

"Hmmm." She seemed contemplative at the answer but didn't dispute it.

"Bronson will be disappointed," She said back to me as she picked up her purse and phone. "Or maybe we will just have to try harder." She pecked at her phone, after which mine beeped signaling a text. "Anyway, you two can figure it out, I need to run." She put her phone in her clutch bag and leaned to me and gave me a peck on the lips. Looking at my phone, she had shared a contact. Bronson M.

"He and his crew are on the regular rotation now," she explained as she headed toward the garage. "He's expecting your call." As she opened the door, she turned back toward me and smiled. "Oh, and Jack. Remember to thank him, until you have the chance to do it personally."

# 19

DIANE AND I WERE HAVING DRINKS and watching Wanda Vision one night later that week, when the doorbell rang. I went and answered it, and when I opened the door, my sister-in-law pushed past, rushing to her sister in the living room, where she started crying with her head in my wife's lap.

"He...he...he..." she struggled to speak or make any sense, but predictably where these sisters were concerned, the problem involved a he. She was crying and shaking so much that she made Diane spill some of her drink, which I was sure disturbed her more than Dana's sobbing. As I went to get one of those bar towels, I kept handy for just such occasions, Dana finished her sentence.

"He left me," she wailed.

"Sean?" Diane asked sounding rather shocked. I was too busy to be shocked as I was using the bar towel to daub the alcohol off my wife's t-shirt, under which were her braless breasts. Finally, after I took what she considered too long to do it, she swatted my hands away and took the towel herself. Meanwhile, Dana ignored her sister's efforts to dry herself and resumed her crying. Finally, my wife took her sister's face and turned it toward her, to try and get her attention.

"Dana," she said in her lawyer's voice, "Why did Sean leave you?" The question seemed gratuitous to me. It could have been any of a number of reasons. Maybe because she was pregnant with another man's child. Maybe because she was sleeping with yet another man. Or maybe it could be because she was in general a scheming, greedy little bitch. So many choices, none of which as it turned out, was correct.

"Not Sean" Dana gasped when she finally regained her voice. "Dan. Dan has left me." That revelation earned me an angry look from my wife. She still blamed me for getting her sister together with the man who then was her first bull. In my defense, I did it so that he would lose interest in my wife. What I didn't know then was Diane was already losing interest in Dan and had set in motion an arrangement that led to what had become a "bullpen by committee." That was working out much better. If you left out the fact that Dan had impregnated my sister-in-law and had now abandoned her, the plan, had been perfect.

"Jack, can you get Dana some water?" I scurried off to avoid my wife's withering gaze as much as to get my sister-in-law water. By the time I returned, Dana was sitting up and using the bar towel to dry her eyes. When she blew her nose in it, I wished I had brought back another. I handed her the water and she actually smiled at me shyly and said thank you. I felt kind of misty myself at her heartfelt expression of gratitude, but the feeling was short-lived when Diane handed me her glass for a refill.

"That's what I need," Dana said, "I need a drink." I looked at Diane, and she looked at me and we both shook our heads and I retreated to fulfill Diane's need for alcohol, a need I felt more sharply due to Dana's visit. So, I retrieved my glass as Diane tried to explain to her sister why drinking is a bad thing for pregnant women and specifically their babies.

She was still explaining when I returned with freshly refilled glasses and water for the expectant mother. Dana was sprawled on the couch with her head in Diane's lap. Placing Diane's Scotch and Dana's water on the coffee table in front of them I started to sit in a chair opposite where they were until my wife caught my eye and motioned me to a spot adjacent to her sister. As Diane stroked Dana's hair gently, I noticed that Dana's "baby bump" had begun to show. Not a lot, but it was becoming noticeable under the tight top she was wearing. I had settled in and taken a long pull of my drink when my wife spoke again in soothing tones.

"Honey," she cooed, "It's going to be okay. You have your family to help you. You have Sean."

Dana made a rather rude sound at the mention of her husband's name. Diane ignored it and continued.

"Where is Sean tonight," she asked. "You told me he got back from San Francisco on Monday. He's not traveling again, is he?" Dana buried her face in the throw Diane had covering her and replied.

"Oh, he's out with Armando again."

Armando? I looked at my wife in amazement and she looked back and shook her head in a movement that was her "not now" move.

"Would you like Jack to rub your feet," Diane asked. Dana's head made a small move that seemed to be a no.

"Are you sure, sweety?" My wife asked again. "It's one of the things he's good at," Then looking at me she grinned her evil grin. "One of the few things." Dana finally wordlessly agreed and after I looked at my wife and stuck my tongue out, I removed my sister-in-law's shoes and began to massage her bare and swollen feet. We sat like that a long time and as we did Dana's body began to get more relaxed to the point of being almost liquid.

"Would you like to stay here tonight?" Diane asked when next she spoke.

"Yes," Dana responded. "Sean won't be home till late. Maybe not at all. I don't want to be alone."

"Then it's settled," Diane told her. "I have some jammies for you, and you can sleep with me tonight. We can snuggle like when we were kids."

"What about . . ." Dana lifted her head and looked at me and asked without finishing the question. I looked at her and smiled an avuncular smile.

"I'll be in the guest room," I told her. "That way you girls can have time together."

"And, breakfast in bed," my wife promised. "When you are ready."

"Goodie," Dana exclaimed "Let's go." She popped off the couch, clearly happier than when she arrived and she scurried to our bedroom with my wife and me trudging wearily behind.

"Armando huh?" I asked Diane when her sister was out of earshot.

"Armando," she repeated back to me, "He's an Argentine."

"A swarthy Latin lover," I said as we walked hand in hand.

"That's something I haven't tried," my wife said contemplatively, almost more to herself than to me.

"Well, don't get any ideas about Armando," I said as we neared the door to our bedroom. "He's taken."

"Yes, he is," she said as we stopped at our room and turned to face me. "And we have learned our lesson about setting people up, haven't we?"

I smiled at her and we kissed.

"Yes," I replied. "Yes, we have."

That made her laugh and we said our goodnights.

"Jack," she said as she went to comfort her sister, "thanks."

I simply nodded and started toward the spare room, where I had learned months before that though we might at times be separate we were "in this" together.

# 20

The next morning (late morning) I was summoned to bring the girls coffee and then breakfast. Dana's mood had lightened and after lunch, she dressed and went back home leaving Diane and me alone again, a situation that I had learned from recent experience would not last long. I also knew because I was my wife's social secretary, scheduling her dates and that night's was with Donald, whom we had begun calling "Iron Horse." Me because he rode a motorcycle, Diane because he was hung like one. As always, we each had our own reasons for all we said and did.

Donald showed up around six, the roar of his Harley heralding his arrival. Diane was still getting ready so I seated him and got him his "drink of choice," Jack Daniels. What followed was several minutes of biker talk that had me mentally begging the floor to open up and swallow me whole, until finally, Diane appeared in a pair of black leather jeans that fit her tighter than the skin on a grape and a matching black leather vest, that barely covered her breasts. She wore nothing under the vest and I was reasonably sure the same could be said for the jeans.

Donald rose to greet her and they embraced and kissed, deeply and for a long time.

"Are you ready?" He asked once they came up for air. Diane replied she was and they went toward the door. I was confused as I watched them leave. Diane looked back and waved and once they go to the bike in the drive, they both climbed on, Diane seated behind Donald and the big black hog thundered away leaving me to wonder and wait.

THE NEXT DAY WAS SUNDAY. It was 9 a.m. and I was on my third cup of coffee when my phone went off.

"Jack!" It was Diane and her voice had a quality I had never heard from her. Desperation. Then relief when I answered as she exclaimed, "Oh my God."

"What's wrong?" I asked because I was always quick with incisive questions.

"You have to come get me," she blurted out. "Please, hurry."

It took me a moment to digest the urgency of the plea. Finally, I asked another of those incisive questions I was so good at.

"Where are you?"

Her answer came more slowly and with more than a hint of sheepishness.

"Jail."

# 21

THE SMALL PRECINCT WAS ABOUT A 40-minute drive from our house, but in reality, it was much farther culturally from our quiet suburban neighborhood. Or a neighborhood that had been quiet until my wife started dragging home men who drove revved-up sports cars with squealing tires and huge Harleys that roared like dragons and broken-down pickups with no mufflers. If this kept up how long would it be before our neighbors surrounded our house carrying pikes and flaming torches? That was one question I did not want to know and an answer I hoped I would never find out.

It was still morning when I pulled up in front of the squat brick building, little more than an hour after Diane and I had talked. It was in what I would have called at one time the "bad part of town." The area was littered with dive bars and biker bars and I had no doubt Donald's basic instinct had called him to his natural habitat. The problem now was he had dragged my wife with him. My wife, a decorated graduate of an Ivy League law school.

The outer office of the police station had a large metal desk, at which sat a rather large severe-looking uniformed woman, who was working at a desktop computer and who didn't look up when I entered.

"Good morning," I said, trying to be pleasant. As soon as I spoke, she held up her hand in a motion indicating I should stop. I did as she finished her task. Once done she looked up and smiled and asked, "What can I do for you?"

I told her who I was and why I was there and she picked up a clipboard and pressed a button and spoke into what looked like an intercom.

"Bring 23763 up. Her husband's here."

I smiled at her again and stood ready to wait. She smiled back with a look I interpreted as, "you poor man." Or maybe I was wrong. Maybe I was projecting because that's how I was feeling about myself.

After minutes which drug like hours, a buzzer sounded and Diane and another woman officer emerged through a heavy looking door at the rear of the room. She looked absolutely terrible. She was wearing an orange jailhouse shirt over her black leather jeans and instead of shoes she had cloth footies. Her head was bowed and her hair looked like it had been styled with a weed whacker. Oh, and she had a black eye. I was still looking at her when the woman at the desk placed her "personal effects" in front of me, which consisted of her clutch bag and one of the two shoes she had been wearing the night before. She said, "There ya go sir." gave Diane several papers to sign and shot me the "you poor man look" again and turned back to her work. She signed and we went to the car.

WE RODE ALMOST THE WHOLE WAY HOME in silence. Me driving and Diane in the fetal position in the passenger seat. Finally, as I was about to turn down our street, Diane sat up and looked at me, and put her hand on my arm.

"Thanks, honey," she said very sincerely. "Thanks for coming to get me."

"What the hell happened Diane?" I felt the anger I had thus far successfully kept under control bubbling up. Diane took her hand off my arm and turned in her seat.

"It was awful and I'll tell you everything that happened," she said in a small voice. "After I've showered and changed." She wrapped her arms around each other and hugged herself.

"Oh, and Jackie," she said without looking at me, "can you make me breakfast while I get cleaned up?

DIANE WAS FRESHLY SHOWERED and sitting at the kitchen counter in her fluffy robe sipping coffee when she finally began filling me in on the gory details. I was nearby poaching eggs and listening intently in both fascination and horror.

"We rode around a while, which was really exciting. I hadn't been on a motorcycle since college." She handed me back her empty cup and I turned from my culinary duties to pour another cup which I subsequently doctored in the way she preferred.

"Thanks, honey," she said as she ingested more caffeine and continued the terrible narrative of her night. "So, we finally ended up at this bar on the west side. Wheelz N Heelz."

"Wheels and heels?" I asked. She shook her head.

"Wheelz N Heelz, with Z's" she corrected me and continued.

"A biker bar," I said venturing a wild guess. Diane nodded and looked impatiently at the eggs I was cooking for her. The toast popped up and I placed it on a plate alongside the butter dish.

"Fix your toast and keep talking," I told her. "Your eggs are almost ready."

Picking up her knife she spread butter on her toast and resumed talking.

"It was just so cool . . . so sleazy, I loved it. All the guys stared at me when we came in," her eyes glowed as she talked and I knew it wasn't the prospect of poached eggs and toast. Even though when I placed the plate in front of her, she dove in ravenously, it didn't slow her reminiscing about the previous night's deep dive at the dive bar.

"How many guys?" I asked anxiously, afraid of where this was leading.

"Oh, fifteen or twenty," she said through a mouthful of toast and eggs. "All in leather and colors. Some really big guys." Looking at me her eyes got very wide. "I mean really big guys."

As reluctant as I was, I felt compelled to ask the obvious question. "How big?"

"BIG," she exclaimed after swallowing.

Diane's eggs and toast were gone but mine sat cooling in front of me, as her story had caused me to lose my appetite. Looking at my plate, she asked, "Are you going to eat those?" I shook my head and pushed my plate to her.

"So," though tension caused my throat to tighten I managed to croak out, "What happened next?"

"Donald got us drinks and a spot at the bar," she said as she devoured my breakfast. "Shots and beers. Bud." She said it making a face, "And whiskey so bad I'm sure they use it to clean the stains off people's teeth." She pushed both now cleaned plates toward me as she continued her story. "But after three rounds, you get used to it."

Gathering the plates, I paused at the sink and decided she had left nothing for me to rinse off, so I placed both directly into the dishwasher and kept listening.

"So, Donald and I were drinking and talking to people. Well, guys. There were a few women there but they didn't talk to me. Finally, Donald took my arm and led me to a small room at the back of the bar."

"Like a storeroom?" I felt the need to contribute to the narration, though my wife did not require the help.

"Yes, a storeroom," she confirmed. "He took me back there and started kissing me. I was getting really drunk. After we kissed for a while. he pushed me to my knees and unzipped his fly. He hadn't closed the door and a few of the guys were watching as I sucked him hard."

None of the details she had related were shocking except one. I had not ever seen Diane drunk in the four years I'd known her. Rarely tipsy. It made me wonder if that contributed to what followed. As she continued to talk. I was certain I was going to find out.

"When he was ready, he turned me away from him and bent me

over an old wooden table in the storeroom. He threw some beer boxes on the floor so I could spread out and then he peeled down my pants."

The thought of my wife bent over and exposed in a dingy room excited me and my cock began to stiffen.

"What then?" I managed to ask when she paused as though lost in thought. The question snapped her back to the present.

"Then he forced his cock into me," she said. "No foreplay, no lube, and because my pants were around my ankles, I couldn't spread my legs. He just rammed right in."

"Ouch," I said sympathetically. "That must have hurt." Finally, she looked at me.

"Oh, baby," she purred. "It hurt so good. He took me and didn't stop till he came. He didn't care that I was squealing like a pig. He did as he pleased." She smiled broadly at the memory and sipped more coffee. Mine was cold in my cup as she continued.

"I was pulling up my pants while Donald was talking to one of the guys. Turk. A white guy with a big belly and a long beard," I filled her cup yet again. I did not want her falling asleep till she had told me all. "Donald came over and told me to be nice to his friends and he went to play pool. The rest is just a blur of cocks and shots, until . . ."

She shook her head and stopped talking for several seconds. I leaned toward her on my stool as though to give her an incentive to continue, which she did, finally.

"I was pretty drunk by then," she admitted. "I remember this woman coming in screaming. One of the guys was her boyfriend. This is how I got this." She put a finger on her black eye and flinched. Whether it was pain or a painful memory I wasn't really sure. Maybe it was both.

"She got me down and was pounding me," Diane explained. "The bitch ripped out the front of my vest and scratched the hell out of my tits." She opened her robe to show me, and sure enough, deep, red slashes marked her breasts. I had never seen a catfight, but now I was seeing the results.

"Finally, Donald must have seen what was happening because he was who pulled her off me," Diane shook her head and covered her face with her hands. "Then all hell broke loose. Guys were fighting, more girls jumped in and I crawled under the table till the cops showed up."

Diane stopped talking for a few minutes. Finally, I could wait no longer and prompted her.

"What then?" I asked.

"They didn't arrest me if that's what you're asking," she replied, though I had already assumed that when I wasn't required to post bond when I picked her up. "They took me to the station to sleep it off. My bag got lost in the shuffle. The bartender found it really late when he was swamping out the place. He got it over to the cops early this morning, so then I could call you."

The answer puzzled me.

"The cops wouldn't let you use the desk phone?" I asked. My wife smiled back at me sheepishly.

"I don't have your number memorized," she answered.

Ouch!

AFTER BREAKFAST, SHE DRESSED IN SHORTS, a discreet top and sandals and we sat together in the backyard and didn't talk much. Finally, later in the day, I made a salad for dinner, which she picked at, her hunger having been sated by two plates of eggs and toast. Then after dinner, I drew her a bath and put in Epsom salts and she lay in the tub soothing her battered body while enjoying a drink.

"Mmmmmm," she said as she lay soaking and sipping, "you never appreciate good whiskey till you have had bad whiskey. Thanks, honey."

"You're welcome honey," I replied as I took a sip of my own scotch. Hers was with soda, while mine was neat. I sat beside the big tub and watched her as she lay back comfortably, letting the warm water wash away the ugliness of the previous 24 hours. I was only partially sad that her motorcycle adventure had turned out so badly. However, it could have been worse. As luck would have it, Diane had a friend of a friend in the county prosecutor's office. Though she hadn't been officially charged we had been worried that news of her "problem" would become public. She had been assured all records of the incident would be buried. So, maybe this had taught her a lesson. Having men in for sex was one thing. Going out and about and being wild with rough men in dangerous places was quite another. So, Donald would be history and we could go back to more civilized bulls like Eugene. The added benefit was no more danger of violating the nuisance provision of our homeowner's association with his noisy bike. Win-win. Or so I thought.

"Well, honey," I said self-assuredly, "It's a shame this didn't work out with Donald."

My wife looked up at me.

"What do you mean?" She seemed confused by the statement.

"Just that I'm sure the whole 'Biker' guy thing was exciting. It's a shame it ended like it did."

"Oh," she said laying her head back again. "It didn't end. I was assured Donald won't be charged. In fact, he's already out."

Now it was my turn to be confused.

"In fact, he's going to be in the regular rotation." She said it as she splashed at the water with her toes playfully. "He and Chet and some of the guys will be coming here. Donald will be expecting you to call and set a date."

## 22

The weeks started to settle into a regular pattern of Eugene, Nathan, Bradley, (who had worked his way back into Diane's good graces by no longer fucking her sister), and the biker gang. Then, one afternoon I was running a dust mop in the living room when I got a call that was a "blast from the past."

"Jack?" I heard a familiar voice say as I answered the phone. "Its Deacon."

After stammering out a hello I waited for Deacon to inform me why he was calling, and wondering what bizarre scene he had in mind this time.

"What night's good for us to get together?" He asked. Diane and he had obviously spoken and it was up to me to squeeze this into her busy social calendar. After clicking into that feature on my phone, I suggested three dates. He chose a week from Wednesday.

"It's a date," Deacon noted breezily and hung up leaving me to wonder, what would he do this time?

It seemed a week from Wednesday came around much quicker than it should, and I spent the day dreading Deacon's visit. Then when my wife arrived home early from the office, I was informed he was not coming to us. We were going to him.

"Are you nervous?" Diane asked as she drove onto the highway headed north past downtown. Looking straight ahead, I replied, quietly, "Kinda." She nodded and smiled mysteriously without taking her eyes off the road.

Deacon had a home in the country. Out away from other homes and perfect for having a horse, planting a garden, or being a serial killer. When Diane parked, I looked around. There was no barn or corral, and no garden. The obvious conclusion caused me to shiver slightly, but still, I exited the car.

"It's a lovely house," Diane said to me as we approached the front door and rang the bell, the sound of which was normal and not an Adams Family like chime. Who would be waiting for us inside? It was, after all, Wednesday.

Instead of a small insane-looking Goethe girl, Deacon answered the door.

"Good evening, folks," the big man said greeting us amiably. "Come on in."

So, we did, with me feeling like a fly going into the parlor of the spider.

Deacon was dressed all in black (of course), and his bald head gleamed as if it were polished. He greeted us and led us toward the back of the house making small talk about our drive over and other trivial seeming subjects that failed to register within my fevered brain. Until finally, we came to a room lined with shelves and hanging clothes and shoes and other items I had not at that point identified. We entered and Diane looked around and oohed and aahed. Until finally I was ushered out by Deacon, to wait.

"Oh, and by the way Jack," he added, "while you wait out here, take off your clothes."

I looked at him blankly, as my wife stood behind him still in awe of the room's contents.

"Take off my clothes?" I said, repeating back to him what I'd been told. Deacon nodded.

"Strip," he told me, "naked." All he got was another of my famous blank looks and me repeating his instruction.

"Naked?" I glanced side to side. "Out here? "He nodded again and closed the door, leaving me to disrobe alone.

It took almost an hour for Deacon to reopen the door. By that time, I had been waiting naked in the hall long enough to feel the chill of the way too cranked up AC and begin to get jittery as to what was to come. Diane was standing behind him and he strode through the doorway as she followed in his wake. At least I thought it was Diane. I was used to my wife in black leather, like her "biker chick" outfit. This was different. This was an intimidating persona. She wore a black leather mask and her breasts were encased in a conical leather bra, and she wore a leather body harness and a black leather g-string. Topping it all off were fishnet hose and 6-inch stilettos. Once she was in the hall, she posed several moments as I stood staring in amazement. Finally, my gaze drifted to Deacon, who watched us both and who was obviously pleased. Finally, I saw she was holding something. Something that looked like a strap, with a buckle on one end. Deacon saw me staring at it and smiled.

"Jack," he said, "do you trust your wife? I mean really trust her?"

I stood silently not knowing how to respond. Of course, I trusted Diane. If I didn't, I'd be on a beach in Tahiti sipping mai tais and would have had no part in the continuing drama our life together had become. Seeing how Diane was dressed and adding to that the fact that I was not, something told me this would require a whole different level of trust.

"Well?" Diane finally asked, "you do, don't you?" I nodded weakly in response, which caused her to smile broadly and Deacon once again to speak.

"In that case kneel and drop your head," He ordered. I did as I was told, surprising no one but myself.

The strap Diane was holding was a collar and when I dropped my head she buckled it around my neck, after which Deacon added a hood to the ensemble. Then a leash was attached to the collar and my wife (at that point my Mistress) led me down a set of stairs to the basement.

Down and down. into the belly of the beast.

# 23

THE BASEMENT HAD AN INDUSTRIAL FEEL, from the lighting to the multiple large rough-hewn apparatuses that occupied most of the space. One was large and X-shaped with rings in what seemed to be strategic spots. Another piece that looked like a sawhorse. That one was padded in black vinyl and alongside it was a similarly cushioned table. There were two sets of cuffs on chains dangling from the ceiling. I shivered as I saw it all and wondered what use they would be put to that night. Instinct told me I would be at least a part of that use.

Diane led me up to a large high-backed chair. Then I realized it was not a chair. It was a throne, and when she stopped us there, she turned to face me, sat, and pointed to a spot at her feet.

"Kneel, slave," she said will all the authority our current situation conferred. A pad had been placed in front of the chair, so I knelt on it and looked at her, and waited. She looked at me and smiled. Though I thought she was trying for a look of evil and menace, there was love there too. Seeing it eased my tension a little, but only a little.

"Good slave," she said then looked towards where I knew

Deacon to be, as though seeking affirmation. He was behind me so I couldn't see his response, but I knew it had been positive, as her smile widened. Her next statement surprised me.

"Kiss my boots, slave," she ordered in her most imperious tone. I had heard it before. She didn't use it often, but she did use it when she really wanted something. My guess was she employed it in this situation for that desired effect. Looking up, she smiled so expectantly and so encouragingly that I as always could not do anything but comply. Bending at the waist, I placed my lips on the shiny, black leather and kissed the toe of each boot. Straightening back to a full kneel, I looked at her expression, which seemed to be that of someone ready to jump up and down and shout "goodie." She didn't, but she was close and I knew I had pleased her. Behind me, I heard Deacon's heavy footsteps go across the concrete floor.

"Come, Mistress Diane," I heard him say. "Bring your slave."

Diane rose from her seat and carefully stepped around me, tugging the leash as she passed. As I began to stand. she snapped her fingers and pointed to the floor, which I understood to mean I was to get on all fours, which I did and crawled along behind her as she dragged me to where Deacon stood, alongside the large, wooden X frame.

I was kneeling, waiting when the big man prompted Diane to have me stand, facing the cross. I got to my feet slowly and did as I was told. Then he got down and put leather cuffs on each ankle. Then he put a similar set on each of my wrists, and I could tell where this was going.

"Lean in," he instructed, and when I complied each of the cuffs was attached to a corresponding ring, until my body was spread in the same approximate shape as the X. Wide and vulnerable. Dreading what might come next.

The cross was up against a back wall, and I was facing that wall, so I couldn't see what Deacon and Diane were doing. For a while, I could hear the sound of footsteps and the thumping and bumping of things being moved and shuffled around behind me. That is until music began to play over the basement sound system. '80s rock. Then I could no longer hear the footsteps and as a result, didn't know where my would-be tormentors were. Until that is, I felt a hand placed unexpectedly on my back, which made me jump, slightly. The gentility of the hand and the sound of the laugh at my nervousness told me it was my wife. She stood behind me for a few seconds that hung like hours until I felt her warm breath, on my left ear.

"Trust me," she whispered, "I'm going to hurt you, but I am not going to harm you."

Then she stepped away from me and as songs changed on the system to one, I recognized.

Carly Simon: "You Belong to Me."

"They're playing our song, honey," she remarked, and then she added, "Be ready."

The impact was a dull thud, rather than a sharp pain. Then again, not something I'd want to experience every day, but not completely unpleasant. After the first five, she stopped for a few minutes and placed her hand once again on my newly tenderized back. She rubbed lightly at first, as though feeling the heat she had created. Then she ran her talon-like nails across the sensitized area, which caused me to gasp and cry out. The cries settled into a series of low groans and plaintive wails. These sounds seemed to please my wife-Mistress. At first, she merely sighed then as I became more vocal, so did she, and I heard her making sounds she usually made during sex. High-keening moans that fueled her to claw my flesh more seriously, until I felt her hand removed from my back and heard Deacon say, "That's enough."

I hung in the cuffs limply and my breath slowed as finally, I was released and collapsed to the basement floor, and quickly felt Diane's arms around me. Holding me. Comforting me. The 'after-care' Deacon had me administer to my wife when she was on the receiving end at our home.

After a short while, I felt much better. More physically comfortable and mentally at peace, and I turned my head, and Diane and I kissed.

"You, okay?" She asked. I replied that I was, and she smiled and loosened her hold on me.

"Then, it's time for you to go sit in that chair over there," she said as she pointed to a comfortable-looking wing chair in the corner. "Because I need a good fucking."

With great effort, I got up and went across the room and sat as Deacon took my wife in his muscular arms and drew her to him. They kissed, passionately and for a long time. Heat radiated from their interaction and as much as I may have wanted to, I couldn't look away. Finally, he broke off the kiss and lifted her, with no visible effort, and carried her across the room to a couch. What may have at one time been called a fainting couch? I was sure Deacon's intent was not to cause Diane to faint. Scream, groan, claw and beg for more was a better guess. He laid her on the fainting couch and carefully removed her outfit. Stripping her of the dominatrix garb, revealing the woman beneath. Then, he proceeded to remove his leathers. The body harness, the heavy boots, then the black leather jeans, until he was standing over my wife completely naked, his impressive physique looming above her. His thick cock hard was dripping as she eyed it greedily. She lay back and splayed her legs, inviting Deacon in, welcoming his sexual plunder. Instead, he stepped to the side and reached and picked something off a side table. Then I saw him tear the foil packet and roll the condom over his stiffened member until it was fully encased. Then he moved back between her spread legs and bent toward her glistening sex and placed the head of his cock at her ready opening, and entered her, slowly. I heard my wife gasp as he slid in fully and he began to piston his hips as he drove in with powerful motions, only to pull out and pound into her again as she screamed in ecstasy and moved in rhythm with his strokes until finally, they orgasmed together, in a deafening cacophony of sound and fury and shared pleasure.

Then, their bodies slowed, their movements became less frantic and soon they were quiet, him still lying on top of her prone body, his cock still fully embedded in her pussy. Finally, he rolled off her and removing the condom threw it and its contents in a nearby wastebasket. Once it was disposed of, he leaned forward and they kissed, which as I watched somehow seemed more intimate than the furor of the sexual excess I had just witnessed. Once the kiss broke off, she lay back and the look on her face showed a certain peace and satisfaction. But as I looked at her, I wondered if she would ever truly be fully sated.

# 24

"How the hell does someone plan a baby shower and why am I responsible for doing it?"

The question seemed rhetorical but as always, I answered, nonetheless.

"Because," I replied patiently, "she's your sister."

"And the father of her child is a man whom I fucked probably a thousand times," she responded tartly. "I managed to avoid getting pregnant. So now since she couldn't I have to throw her a party?"

I ignored the comment for two reasons. First, because I was busy working on the guest list, and secondly, I didn't want it to be pointed out to me again that I had been largely responsible for the union of Dana and her sperm donor and that it would in a few short months bear fruit. By pointed out I mean I did not want my nose rubbed in that fact yet again. So, I steadily tended to the details of the soiree as that job had fallen to me. Diane was shouldering the task of bitching about it, something she seemed to warm to with enthusiasm.

"Does your mom have any suggestions?" I asked. My wife shrugged. It was an elegant shrug, but a shrug, nonetheless.

"Call her and ask her," she replied. "I'm tired of talking to her about the whole baby thing. That doesn't end well anymore."

I nodded. Similarly, I wanted to avoid the subject with Sheila, who seemed to blame me for depriving her of a grandchild from her older daughter. Little did she know my key role in facilitating the production of the one her younger daughter was presently gestating. For my own health and safety, I hoped those facts never came to her attention.

"Maybe we should just ask Dana," I suggested, though my sister-in-law was now almost as risky to talk with as my mother-in-law, due to a combination of morning sickness and sexual deprivation. Dan was assiduously avoiding the mother of his child and Bradley had sworn off having carnal knowledge of her at the insistence of my wife and the promise he could get back into the "rotation." He did and by an odd coincidence was scheduled to pay her a conjugal visit that very night.

AROUND 9 P.M. WE HEARD A RUMBLING coming up our dive.

"Either Bradley here or the Hindenburg has landed again," I joked as I started to the door.

"If cheapskate Dan would give him a raise, maybe he could afford a muffler," Diane suggested as she began to undress in preparation for what was usually a hurried visit by this particular bull. I would have said his sessions were "wham bam and thank you, ma'am," except he was often in such a hurry to return to work that he forgot to say thank you.

"You could suggest the raise," I joked. "That way he might have a chance of getting it." My wife laughed.

"More likely, he'd have a suggestion as to a use of my tailpipe," she replied. "And frankly I wouldn't fuck him with your asshole."

With that remark hanging in the air, I headed to the front door, feeling strangely comforted, and strangely not.

BRADLEY WAS PUTTING ON HIS BLACK DRESS SLACKS again and tucking in his shirt less than 30 minutes later. He seemed quite happy and satisfied. Diane, however, was less so.

"That was brief," She commented snarkily.

"Well," I said trying to be of comfort, "they say brevity is the soul of wit." Diane gave me one of her withering looks that I knew all too well.

"It's not the soul of dick," she replied testily. "If this keeps up, I'll give him back to Dana."

"Might be for the best," I agreed. "It might improve her mood."

Diane sat on the edge of the bed and put on her fluffy white robe. Then she took my hand and we walked toward the living room.

"You don't want to shower?" I asked. She laughed.

"What just happened didn't make me work up a sweat," she replied. "Donald, for all his faults, is pretty damn good at keeping . . ." covered up," so he didn't get any . . . you know, on me."

"It's why he gets such great tips," I joked. "Husbands tip better when a bull doesn't get cum on the wife."

"In the absence of passion, neatness counts," she said agreeably as she settled onto the couch. "Honey, can you get me a drink?"

I was already headed toward the bar by the time she asked.

"Thank you, honey," she called behind me.

She smiled when I came back with her scotch and soda. She sipped it with greater pleasure than her earlier sexual foray with Bradley.

"Play your cards right mister, and you might just get lucky later on," she said it while giving me her "come hither" look that I didn't see very often. At least, directed at me. She took another long pull of her drink, and once again spoke.

"Who's up next on my dance card, honey?" I picked up my phone and looked at the calendar.

"Eugene on Friday, Donald and the bikers on Saturday, and if they run in their usual form they will spill over into Sunday."

"Do you have enough beer for them?" Diane asked.

"No," I answered. "But then no one does. If they keep coming, I'll need to get a distributorship."

"The true test is can they keep me cumming, isn't it?" Diane giggled and sipped more scotch. "The answer so far has been yes."

I kept scrolling through the calendar.

"Bronson's out of town the next two weeks," I pointed out. Diane looked at me in disappointment. Her expression made my cuckold anxiety flare, as I had begun to fear my wife was becoming attached to the young, sexy black man in the same way as she had gotten cock struck with Dan.

"The good news is," I added quickly. "I managed to get reservations at that new restaurant downtown for when he gets back." Her face brightened and she emptied her glass and placed it on the end table. I reached to get it, to give her a refill. She grasped my wrist and shook her head.

"Let's not," she said. "Unless you have forgotten what I said before about getting lucky."

I assured her I had not forgotten and took her hand.

"Deal me in," I said as we hurried hand in hand to the bedroom.

# 25

It was soon after I'd gotten the ten cases of beer on ice that the bikers started to arrive. I could only wonder what the neighbors thought as ten noisy motorcycles pulled into our drive and parked, and what they would think when they were all still there the next day. All day. Would they be gathering their torches and sharpening their pikes? Would we be escorted out of the development on the unwelcome wagon?

Once the guys were there, I had no time to contemplate such existential questions. I was too busy passing out beer and snacks and wondering how I'd get the wing sauce and ground-in pork rinds out of the living room carpet.

It took less than a full beer before one of the bikers had his pants down and Diane's skirt up, fucking her as she leaned on the back of the sectional, while the other nine men alternated watching them, drinking beer, and checking out the MMA action on the big screen. Then, as the first man and my wife were in mid-fuck another stood and unzipped his fly in direct proximity to her face, and more specifically waiting mouth. As soon as his hardened cock was free, she engulfed it in her mouth, and he took hold of her head and began pumping her face with a steady rhythm that seemed to coordinate well with the man who was fucking her cunt. Others in the gathered throng leered at the spectacle admiringly.

"Mmmm," one said to no one in particular. "That's nice." Then another asked me if I had ever seen her "spit-roasted" and once I thought about it, I realized I had not. It was a fascinating spectacle and I hated to admit I stared fixedly as the two men came hard in each end of the woman I loved. Finally, my concentration was broken as the trio disengaged and the man who had face fucked her requested another beer.

"Thirsty work huh?" I remarked as I hurried away to fetch him another cold one. When I returned Diane's lips encircled another man's stiff member and still another was lined up behind her.

"She ever take it up the ass?" He was asking me because my wife was obviously too busy to answer. He was big, with a large belly, but also well-endowed with a cock that matched his physique. When we had been introduced earlier, I'd learned his name was Chet. There was a time I would have called a man like Chet fat. That was a time before I feared death at his hands. So, at this point, I would call Chet, and his cock both thick.

"Y-yes," I stammered in reply. That made him smile and point to the side table.

"Hand that over, okay, bud?" He was asking me for the bottle of water-based lube I had placed there before the onslaught. Good cucks are like boy scouts. Always prepared. As I went to pass the bottle to him, he instead spread his hands. He wanted to squirt the lubricant on his open palms, which I did. Once I had emptied an amount to his liking he took his cock, which was already out of his pants, and rubbed it up and down, till it was glistening and slick. Then, he placed the head, at my wife's small, tight hole and, moving his hips, began to push. I heard a gasp escape her lips around the cock, she was servicing orally. Gradually, more gently than I would have guessed from a man of his size, he inserted himself, until he was balls deep. He ground his hips powerfully against the milky white half-moons of her ass, and she groaned as much as was possible with her mouth so full. Then he started going in and out of her in short strokes as the man at her head, unlike the previous one she'd sucked stayed remarkably still, letting her do all the work. She seemed up to the task and quickly he exploded in her mouth as she milked him of every drop. Even a few that dripped down her chin, that she scooped onto her fingertip, which she then licked clean. Finally, the big man behind her finished in her ass, grunting and thrusting and rocking her forward as she squealed in delight. Then, both disengaged from her, and like a game of kinky musical chairs, two more of the bikers replaced them.

When each man had taken a turn at my wife, they collapsed in various places around the living room, drinking beer and watching an auction of expensive cars that had replaced the mixed martial arts competition after its conclusion.

Then the crowd began to thin out, with a few of the guys saying they had to,, "Get home to the old lady." The roaring of the departing hogs seemed to revive those who had remained and each of those who were left taking another turn, though each did it singly this time. All but Donald, who sat quietly and drank his beer. He watched as his remaining six buddies used Diane's pussy and asshole in turn and sat back down to finish the remaining snacks and drink more beer, the supply of which they had greatly diminished.

Finally, the last man's cock fell out of my wife with a noisy plop. It was the big guy that had been the first to take her ass. Since variety is the spice of life, he fucked her pussy this time. He climbed from between her legs with great effort and was hiking up his jeans as Donald rose to his feet and clapped his hands, twice.

"Funs over," he announced. "Time to go." His friends looked at him with as much shock as you can from behind beer goggles. He looked at each and made a hurrying gesture and they grudgingly got out of their comfortable seats and trudged wearily toward the door. Diane, meanwhile, was still in the process of coming out of her sex-induced haze and was just beginning to realize what was going on. I was too, but unlike my wife, I was grateful for the house to empty out so I could get to bed. Looking at the time on my phone made me even more tired. It was 3:36 a.m. Diane was bewildered and as she came to was on the verge of getting upset at what was being done. I knew the indicators, as I had been seeing them for four years. She was also not completely sexually satisfied, something I had also seen for four years. I was in the process of ushering the biker gang to the door and my wife was in the process of dragging her battered and well-used body off the sofa to object when Donald, whom it was obvious was not leaving with his friends went to Diane and roughly grabbed her wrist. Then without as much as a look in my direction, he dragged her down the hall toward our bedroom, naked and stumbling to stay on her feet. He threw her into the room and followed her in, noisily slamming the door after them.

What followed was a series of banging and screaming and yelling and swearing that was extreme even by the standards established by my wife the last several months. Diane had shown she liked rough sex, but what was happening seemed beyond the pale, and I stood outside my bedroom terribly conflicted as to whether or not I should intervene. The loudest, most violent-sounding crash yet made the decision for me, and I threw open the door to the scene of my naked wife sitting on our bed over the prone body of her would-be lover. His pants were around his ankles and pieces of what had been a table lamp were scattered on the comforter around him.

"Let's get him out of here," Diane told me, and she got up and off the bed and went to get her robe.

"Pull up his pants," she said as she wrapped herself in the fluffy robe that I had recently laundered. As I did as I was told, I was sure accomplishing the task was easier than it would have been when Donald left the living room with my wife in tow, and I pulled his jeans up past his shriveled cock and buckled his belt. Once he was redressed so as not to offend the sensibilities of the general public, I grabbed under the biker's armpits and Diane took his legs and we carried him through the house.

"Just be glad," Diane said as we strained to get the Donald down the hall, "that this isn't Chet."

I grunted in agreement and when we finally reached the front door, we deposited the insensible Donald out on the front stoop.

It was a little past 4:30 and I was cleaning the broken lamp off the bed as Diane sat in my chair supervising my work.

"Don't get too used to sitting there," I joked as I picked up the shattered pieces so we could sleep without sustaining life-threatening injuries.

"No worries there," my wife replied. "What would I have to watch even if I did?"

"Good point," I agreed as I got the last few bits off the bedclothes.

"So," I asked finally, "What the hell happened? Did he get too rough for you? Was he violent? Should I have stepped in?"

Diane leaned back in my chair and reached and clasped her hands behind her head. She was thinking. Finally, she responded.

"The answers," she said sleepily, "are, no, no, and no."

I placed the wastebasket aside and sat on the edge of the now-clean bed and listened. We sat there until my curiosity got the better of me and I repeated my question.

"So, what the hell happened?"

My wife smiled before she answered.

"He thought he was boss," she said simply. "He tried to 'Dan' me."

I looked at her and tipped my head slightly like dogs do when they see something that interests them.

"You mean when he cleared the other guys out?" I asked. Diane nodded.

"He got territorial," she answered, "and that's not acceptable anymore. No matter how big their dicks are."

Having said that, I sat watching her. Even worn out and covered in other men's cum, she was still the same beautiful, powerful woman I'd married, and at that moment I loved her and respected her more than the day we met. Pulling back the covers, I patted her spot in our bed. Taking the hint, she got up from the chair and we lay down together.

"So," I said sleepily "Tonight was our first and only biker bang?"

Diane raised her head off her pillow and gave me her usual look indicating I had said something stupid.

"Not at all," she replied, laying back down. We held each other a long time until finally, she spoke before drifting off to sleep.

"After all, I have Chet's number."

# 26

"It's a lovely party, Diane." My wife and I listened as her mother gushed praise on her daughter about the baby shower I had been solely responsible for arranging.

"You are so talented, dear," she continued. "With all the other responsibilities you have. It's amazing. You are amazing."

"Aww, thanks, mom." Diane replied beaming. "Jack, helped a little." She patted my arm condescendingly as she said it. Despite that fact, I smiled, appreciative of the scrap of praise thrown my way.

Dana and Sean were at the bar. Together, surprisingly enough. So, Diane and I drifted over in their direction, leaving Sheila to talk to an uncle who had flown in from Chicago for the event.

"Thanks again," Sean said graciously, addressing his statement to us both. Dana stood alongside her husband sipping a club soda, though she seemed to be doing both with no enthusiasm.

"You are so welcome," Diane replied proving once again how graciously she could accept praise for my efforts. "It seems like everyone's having a good time."

I surveyed the room and realized I knew everyone there, except one young man. Hispanic. Swarthy and handsome, with a trim physique that was obvious even beneath his expensive suit. My wife noticed my questioning look as we left the "happy couple" to go to where I had placed the hors devoeres. She nodded and mouthed the word," Armando."

Diane took a small plate and got a variety of finger foods before wandering toward her brother-in-law's paramour. I followed closely behind, both fearful of and intensely curious about what she intended to do.

"Good afternoon," she said politely, "I'm Diane, and this is my husband Jack." The young man offered his hand and I took it and we shook hands.

"I'm Armando," he replied. "I'm a friend of Sean's."

Diane nodded without comment. As I watched her, I realized I had seen that look from her in court, during cross-examinations. Had Armando known her better he would have been afraid. He didn't, so it was that whole "welcome to my parlor" thing again.

"A work friend?" She asked leadingly. "A sports friend?"

"Sean doesn't play sports," Armando replied nervously. He was starting to realize he was being trapped. For her part, Diane kept smiling and speaking in her calm steady "lawyer's voice." Because of that, she was attracting no more attention from the rest of those at the shower than if she was discussing the weather or the latest movie with the unfortunate Armando.

"Oh, that's not what I've heard," she said evenly. "I've heard he likes to play with balls."

Despite his swarthy complexion, the young man seemed to blush, and I thought I could see beads of sweat begin to form on his handsome face.

"What's the point of this?" Armando asked, lowering his voice.

"The point is," my wife said still maintaining her lawyer's voice, "this is my sister's party. To celebrate her and her baby. You, therefore, have no place here, and indeed your presence could in fact cause her discomfort. That's something I mean to prevent."

Armando tried to look back at Diane defiantly. Doing that was hard. I'd tried it myself. There weren't many times when I had succeeded. Armando failed miserably and so instead, he looked away but said testily. "What are you going to do about it? Get your husband to throw me out?"

Armando looked at me, with a look that was meant to be derisive. Little did he know I'd experienced so much derision it no longer affected me. At least not in a negative way.

"No," Diane replied in a voice so calm it had a tinge of sweetness. "But, I have other men I can call. Big, tough guys. If they threw you out of here, they wouldn't do it as nicely as we will."

Armando winced slightly but put up both hands with the palms facing Diane. It was a gesture of surrender.

"I'll leave," he said and turned and headed to the door. As he left, I noticed he and Sean exchange looks, but he departed without saying any more to anyone. Once he was gone Dana smiled at her sister and Diane smiled back. Then she popped a canape in her mouth and chewed with less ferocity than she had just chewed Armando's ass.

"I didn't invite him," I said, intending to build my defense. My wife swallowed, smiled, and shook her head.

"Sean did," she explained. "Dana and he had a huge fight over it. She was hoping he wouldn't come."

"But you handled it," I said admiringly. She laughed.

"Of course, darling," she replied. "In case you haven't noticed I'm good at handling men coming and going."

I couldn't help but laugh at her bad joke, though after I did, I looked around self-consciously, realizing no one noticed.

"The best ever," I told her. "In every sense of the meaning."

She took the last appetizer off her plate and fed it to me. I took it and ate it with relish.

"Now, husband," She said, "I need another drink. Planning this party and throwing people out of it is thirsty work."

## 27

"**W**HAT TIME ARE WE MEETING BRONSON?" Diane asked me anxiously as she carefully applied the makeup that I knew would be smeared beyond repair by raucous sexual congress later on that night.

"Seven o'clock for drinks. Our dinner reservation is for 8," I answered patiently. I said it as I shaved. I once had tried for the "stubbly" look preferred by so many of the men my wife lusted after, but she quickly put a stop to it, explaining to me the difference between young and stubbly and old and scruffy, and that unshaven, I was the latter. So, I made sure I was shaved at all times thereafter.

"How does this look?" She asked after she slipped into a dress that at one time, I would have considered way too short and far too low cut. As we were meeting her young black lover whom she had not seen in weeks it was perfect. I also noted and didn't comment on the fact that before she "slipped into" her dress, she did not slip on any lingerie, knowing that fact would save time and laundry later.

"Did you get a new box of condoms?" Diane asked. I responded that I had.

"Good," she said, "because at my gyno appointment the week before last, she noted some blood pressure issues I've been having, so she took me off the pill."

"You've been off it since then?" The thought was scaring me, but my wife shook her head dismissively.

"It's fine as long as I use condoms till I'm back on, which I have and which I will again tonight," she explained. "You got Magnums, right?" I assured her I had. She smiled.

"Good," she said, "Because Bronson is definitely a Magnum kinda guy."

We arrived downtown at 6:47, stepping out of the Volvo sedan that had Ubered us there. The bar was crowded but a bribe, to the maitre de, secured us a small table out of the traffic pattern where we ordered drinks and sat waiting for Bronson to be fashionably late.

He finally arrived at 7:30. Not that I was counting the minutes. I was enjoying time with my wife when her dashing lover of the moment breezed in, in a trendy black suit and a gleaming white shirt. No tie (of course). He greeted me briefly then went to Diane to begin the evening's seduction.

"Diane," he gushed, "It's always too long to be apart." Then they kissed in a way that was far too intimate for a man to kiss a married woman in a public place. I had gotten used to it, so I ignored the attendant humiliation of my wife getting a public tonsillectomy from a sexy younger man. Harder to overlook was that he sat on the other side of the table and Diane changed seats to be beside him.

"How's my baby been?" I heard Bronson say. The question obviously meant for Diane and not for me, so I didn't answer. Diane did, outlining in vivid detail the minutiae of her life while the man who was now the focus of her attention had been away. Included in this was the incident with Armando at Dana's baby shower, which made Bronson laugh harder than the humor of the situation warranted.

"You are a tigress," he declared when his laughter died down which caused her to make a face and go, "GRRRRRRR," and led to gratuitous groping while I sat and watched along with most of the other bar patrons. After the groping they kissed again, which attracted yet more attention, which was perhaps what Bronson desired, but which I definitely did not.

Finally, after more kissing, fondling, and handholding in which I was not a participant, the maitre de came to tell us our table was waiting. If I expected that to alleviate the sexual tension (I did not), I would have been sadly disappointed. They sat on the same side of the table across from me and held each other, fed each other, and showed intimacy in ways that were only barely street legal. We managed to make it through dinner without having the vice squad called, and after dessert, we headed for our house in another Uber, and by we, I mean Bronson, Diane, and me. Me in the front, Bronson and Diane in the backseat together doing things so distracting that the poor driver almost had a wreck. When we finally arrived, I doubled the tip and he thanked me and said he hoped I would have a nice night. He didn't add that he was sure they would but I could tell he was thinking it, as he drove away.

Once we were in the house, Diane and Bronson wasted no time tearing each other's clothes off and by the time I brought in the drinks they were naked and my wife was sucking her lover's long, ebony shaft on the sectional in preparation for the main event, or perhaps I should say events, which we all expected to be multiple sessions of fucking.

Then, something none of us expected happened. The doorbell rang. It was startling in that it was after 11 o'clock. Bronson and Diane ceased amorous activities and the three of us looked at each other.

"Who could it be?" Diane asked, obviously annoyed at the unexpected interruption. I shrugged.

"Maybe the driver wants to see the rest of the show," I commented as I started for the door. "Only one way to find out. But you two should probably cover-up."

When I opened the door Dana was waiting impatiently. She pushed past me and hurried into the living room where Bronson had barely had time to pull on his boxer briefs. Dana stopped and took in the view and hardly noticed her sister clutching her dress in front of her in a vain attempt at decency. Dana's eyes widened and Bronson, by then fully in his underwear made no attempt to put on his pants, seeming to enjoy the admiring gaze of a new onlooker.

"Dana!" My wife screamed in indignation as her sister continued to ogle the nearly naked Bronson. Bronson, for his part, leaned back on the sofa to give Dana a better view. Meanwhile, my wife was fumbling with her dress and not successfully I might add. Finally, I took pity on her and went to our bedroom and got her robe, and threw it to her, at which point she hurriedly wrapped herself in it. As she was doing that, her sister came and sat on the sectional, still staring at that night's object of Diane's sexual desire.

"Put your pants on," Diane told Bronson with considerable force, but her young lover ignored her demand and spread his legs so the bulge in his shorts was even more prominent. Dana stared and licked her lips hungrily.

"Don't do that on my account," she told him. "I'm Dana, by the way."

"I'm Bronson" he replied and got up, went over, and took Dana's hand, and kissed it tenderly which made Dana giggle like a schoolgirl. Bronson held Dana's hand and seemed to be caressing it as their eyes locked on each other. Diane cleared her throat noisily, twice. Bronson took the hint after the second time and released his grip but went over to sit next to Dana. Meanwhile, I watched as my wife indignantly crossed her arms over her chest. If this had been a cartoon steam would have been rising off her. So, I did what any supportive husband would do given the situation. I went to make myself a drink.

When I returned Bronson and Dana were chatting casually while Diane continued watching and angrily hugging herself. Her drink sat on the coffee table untouched. Since it appeared Bronson wasn't going to move anytime soon, I went and sat in the spot he vacated beside my wife.

"So," Bronson asked, "How far along are you, Dana?"

"Nearly seven months," she explained and went on to explain the many joys of her pregnancy. Diane rolled her eyes and, tasting her drink, made a face and looked at me with disgust.

"That's terrible," she said testily. I shrugged.

"It wasn't an hour ago," I said defensively. She handed me her glass.

"Can you get me a fresh drink?" Then she hurriedly added, "Honey." to the demand. I looked at my half-empty glass, finished the drinking process, and took my wife's and departed to get us both refills. As I left, I heard Bronson say to my sister-in-law, "I just think pregnant women are so sexy," and decided I might not go back.

I did, and when I returned Bronson was alone, still in his underwear, sitting unashamedly in his skin-tight boxer briefs. Not that he had any reason to be ashamed, judging from the way the stretchy material hugged his considerable endowment. He was sipping his by now watery drink. His standards must not be as high as Diane's. Or maybe he doubted I'd get him a fresh one since he was there to fuck my wife. The thought made me chuckle. The kid's got a lot to learn about cuckolds.

"Where are the girls?" I finally asked. Bronson pointed to the hallway.

"They went to talk," he said. That bit of information filled me with a sense of dread. Surely Diane wouldn't hit a pregnant woman, even if that woman was her sister. Then I remembered how my wife got when she was sexually frustrated and considered it possible.

"I'd better go check on them," I told Bronson, though I wasn't sure he heard me, or if he heard me, if he cared.

"Dana, sweetie I do care, but you have to be reasonable." My wife was pleading with her sister to be reasonable. Given my experience with Dana, she would have better hope of success pleading with the sun to rise in the west.

"Sissy." Dana said to her sister, "You don't understand. It's been so long."

Diane's head dropped to her considerable chest and she shook it in sad defeat.

"Alright," she declared, "Alright, but just this once." Dana clapped her hands happily and ran back toward the living room as fast as a seven-month pregnant woman could run, passing without so much as a word. Once she had gone, I looked questioningly at my wife.

"She and Bronson are going to . . ." she told me disgustedly. "You know."

Whether fortunately or unfortunately, after all this time and the countless debaucheries, yes, I certainly did know, so I continued to sip my drink without comment, as we went together to the living room to see what the plan was.

When we got there, Dana was sitting on Bronson's lap with her top off, her milk-filled breasts still covered by her bra, but with Bronson rubbing her swollen and exposed belly.

"You're okay with this?" Bronson asked my wife, who nodded wordlessly. Her agreement made him smile broadly.

"You know, I have always dreamed of having sisters together," he said. His relating that desire caused Diane to screw her face into a most unpleasant expression and go, "Ewwwwwwww. NO!"

"Hmmm," Bronson said turning his attention back to Dana and her belly. "I never knew your sister was such a prude." Dana giggled.

"That's okay, handsome. We can make our own fun without the old lady." As she said it, she pulled his face to hers and they kissed. Once their kiss broke, Dana leaped to her feet, pulled Bronson off the couch, and dragged him toward the hall.

"Dana," Diane shouted after her fleeing sister and erstwhile lover. "Remember, the guest room. Like we agreed."

BUT, A FEW MINUTES LATER, AFTER I HAD GOTTEN MY WIFE and I new drink Dana came back into the living room, clad only in her panties, with her arms covering her swollen breasts.

"Sissy," she said meekly. "The bed in that room is so small . . ." The implicit request made Diane throw up her hands in surrender.

"Fine," she told her near-naked sibling, who exited hurriedly. "But do not mess up the sheets," she called after her.

We sat finishing our drinks as we heard the door slam and raucous laughter filter down the hall. Diane shook her head sadly.

"This evening didn't turn out quite the way you planned did it, sissy?" I asked my wife, who scowled at me.

"Call me that again," she said sourly, and I'll get the French maids outfit and we'll see who the sissy really is."

The threat made me gulp the remainder of my Scotch and put the glass on the end table.

"Time to turn in, sweetheart?" I asked meekly.

"JACK," DIANE MOANED DEJECTEDLY, "This bed is so small."

Our bodies were pressed together in the bed in the spare room where I had spent many a night in the Dan era. Before the cuckold chair. Before I was allowed to watch as multiple men defiled the body of the woman I married. As we lay there, I wondered if the sounds of passion coming from our bedroom and not the size of our sleeping area were the source of her unhappiness.

"Just relax and go to sleep," I advised. "I'll move over." Which I did, at the risk of falling off the edge. Surprisingly when I did, she reached and pulled me closer to her.

"No, don't," I was told. However, she lay there holding me and not sleeping as the sounds of love next door became louder and more insistent.

"So," she began, "you slept in here a lot. How did you do it?"

"Well," I pointed to my underwear-covered crotch and made an up-and-down motion with my hand. "That helped a lot."

She raised her eyebrows and gave a nod. Then without another word, she sat up and took off her robe, then pulled down my underwear, and my cock, which was by then hard, sprang forth, in all its diminutive glory.

"Hmmm," she said contemplatively. "Someone's excited. Does listening always have that effect?"

"Yes," I confessed, "though having you here with me makes me more so."

She smiled and lowered her head and took my cock in her

mouth, and I personally experienced what I for so long had only watched. Then after she got me as hard as was possible, she released her oral grip on my member and straddled me and scooted till her pussy engulfed my cock and she rode me cowgirl style. We listened to the noise being made by Dana and Bronson and our own movements took on the same rhythmic patterns and we began to moan almost as loudly until the two rooms became almost a battle of the bands which culminated in four cataclysmic orgasms, simultaneous and volcanic after which we all got quiet, and Diane and I drifted off to sleep.

A FEW HOURS LATER I AWOKE in the small bed alone. In the bedroom next door, I could hear sounds once again. Passionate sounds. Sexual sounds. Sounds that made me wonder where my wife had gone. The bathroom perhaps? Or had she reconsidered her revulsion to sexual congress involving her sister and the young black stallion? I got out of bed and pulled on my underwear and quietly went out to the hall bath. No, Diane. None of the smoke alarms had gone off, so she was not making breakfast. That left one possibility. Creeping down the hall I stood at our bedroom door and placed an ear to it, to better listen. There were voices. People's voices raised, in the joys of sexual excess and bedsprings. The sounds of vigorous intercourse. But was it three people? There was only one way to know. Slowly, and against my better judgment, I opened the door.

Diane was on the bed, on all fours and Bronson was pounding her pussy doggie style, as she squealed in delight. Finally, he came with a noisy roar accompanied by her moaning loud and long, then, as Bronson pulled out an exclamation by him.

"Oops," he said sheepishly. "We broke the condom."

WE?

Then I heard my wife exclaim, "Oh shit!"

It was at that point I hurriedly closed the door so as not to be seen, but once I was back in the spare room alone the realization struck me like a thunderbolt. Bronson had just cum in my wife's unprotected pussy, and the night before, I had as well. As I was weighing the consequences the door opened and Diane peeked in.

"Great," she said smiling, "You're awake."

"Yeah," I said rubbing my eyes sleepily. "Just woke up."

Her smile broadened.

"Dana left early, so I thought I would go visit Bronson," she explained. "We wondered if you'd fix us breakfast."

"Sure," I replied agreeably. "Give me a minute."

"No hurry," she said. "Coffee first?"

"Gotcha," I said and smiled at her, as she closed the door to return to her lover. When she was gone, I wondered if I needed to put the almond milk in hers this morning. After all Bronson and I had already provided her with plenty of cream.

# 28

"You worry too much," my wife scolded me. "I'm sure your swimmers are well past their expiration dates and besides, what makes you think you got deep enough in me to plant any?" Then she laughed, not knowing that I knew Bronson's balloon had popped inside her. His "swimmers" were young and strong and he definitely got deep enough for implantation.

So, I had to sweat out waiting and hoping against hope that no seeds had taken root that night. Over the course of several weeks, I would casually mention my concerns and she would seem annoyed with me and brush them aside as needless and we went about the business of our lives intermingled with her diverse sex life that now included not only Eugene and Bradley and occasionally Nathan and Tim, but also Chet and several men from the biker group, though not Donald. Bronson seemed not to have lost his access, although he continued fucking her sister. He continued to pursue the idea of a threesome with Dana and Diane, something that as perverse as she could be at times, my wife was unwilling to do. As I had noted on previous occasions, she might be a slut, but she was an ethical slut. Yet, despite those obvious conflicts, Bronson retained his sexual access. Why?

Then, one day after I had stopped obsessing, I found something that was profoundly disturbing and was a clue as to the why of that question. It was on a Thursday and Diane had gone to the office early that day for a client meeting. While cleaning the bathroom I came across something that shook me to my core. It was a pregnancy test. I hadn't seen one in almost 30 years, since my first wife used them before our children came along. Even then they confused me. The presence of such a test in my house showed that as much as she had dismissed my worries about an unintended pregnancy, Diane was worried too.

Looking at it, I tried to discern if it had shown a result. I wondered what the symbols meant. The packaging was gone, so I couldn't read the instructions. So as a man. I needed someone to interpret them. I found myself wishing I had paid closer attention years ago. Instead, I was overly concerned with such work issues as actuary tables. Maybe that could be said of all aspects of my previous marriage. The thought occurred to call Elizabeth, my first wife to ask. The thought passed quickly when another thought occurred, that asking my first wife if my second wife was pregnant might just be a tad bit awkward.

So, I did the next best thing. I put the test in my pocket and drove to the nearest drug store. Surely the druggist would know.

SHE DID, THOUGH FINDING THE ANSWER INVOLVED a small measure of abuse and humiliation, but those were things I'd become accustomed to in my new life.

"Can you tell me what this means?" I asked, pulling the test out of my pocket. The druggist took it from me and looked.

"Is this your granddaughters?" She asked. It seemed to be a serious question. Though I tried to ignore the implication.

"No," I replied indignantly. "If you must know, it's my wife's."

She looked at it again.

"Why don't you ask your wife?" She responded with a sensible question to what was an absurd situation.

"Because I think she's trying to surprise me," I replied in exasperation, "and before you ask, I don't like surprises."

She handed it back and looked at me closely and smiled again. "Well, surprise," she said, "Looks like you're going to be a daddy."

I took the device from her, thanked her, and walked away, thinking, well maybe not me, but somebody was going to be a daddy.

# 29

Somehow, I made it home without driving into a wall. I was so distracted that was a distinct possibility. Diane was pregnant, and she knew she was pregnant and hadn't told me. Those facts seemed to indicate her supposition was the same as mine. The baby's father was Bronson. It only made sense. He was younger. Stronger. His sperm figured to be stronger and more vital. Maybe she knew already and was trying to figure out how to break the news to me. Not only did I not know how a pregnancy test worked, I understood even less about DNA. But, as I tried to safely make it home, I decided it was a good time to find out.

So, I did. God bless you Google. Turned out tests to determine the DNA of a fetus could not be performed till the 16th week of pregnancy. Diane was less than 7 weeks along, so we would have at least 9 more weeks of wondering.

Once I got to the house, I put the test back where I'd found it, and went about my usual tasks, which I had trouble doing because of my anxiety, which grew exponentially as the day wore on. Thoughts raced through my mind and most weren't happy thoughts for me. Could I raise another child? I thought that phase of my life was behind me. How would Diane respond? She had never been a mother before and when the issue came up, she literally got the heaves.

Then there were the paternity issues. Could I raise another man's child? What would Bronson do? Would he sue for visitation? For custody? He seemed to enjoy the benefits of "no strings" sex, but fatherhood was different. A child is not an abstract and more than once has changed a man's feelings.

Then the contemplation of feelings led me to wonder about my wife. Her feelings about the father of her child. Once Bronson had taken up with Dana, I thought Diane would reject him as she had Bradley under similar circumstances. She had not and had sex with him as soon as her sister was out the door, which is what led us into this mess. As I thought my fevered brain raced to the realization, she was still fucking him even after realizing she was pregnant. Was that a factor attracting her to the handsome, charming young man?

A text beeped in on my phone, and having read it I was hit with the fact that she was going to continue.

Diane: *Hi Honey. If we have plans tonight, cancel them, please. I'll be with Bronson.*

THE UNEXPECTED SCHEDULE CHANGE HAD ME scrambling. I called Chet, who was going to be with us that night, and apologized profusely. Lying I said Diane was sick. When he pressed me as to what was wrong, I said she was throwing up, he jokingly said, "She ain't pregnant is she?"

I tried to work up a laugh and failed, so finally I lied again and told him, of course not. Luckily, he seemed to believe me and said he'd call the gang. I assured him we'd reschedule when she was feeling better. I didn't tell him it might take another seven months.

Having performed my cuckold duty, the rest of the day I busied myself with the role of househusband. Then at 5:45, my wife's car pulled into the garage. She quickly came into the house, giving me a peck on the cheek, rushed to the bedroom. I had poured her a welcome home club soda. Shortly thereafter she came down the hall in a "barely there" dress and shoes she had once called," Fuck me pumps" gulped down her club soda and made a face as she headed for the door.

"Diane," I called after her, "can't we take a minute to talk?" I pleaded.

She looked at me blankly and smiled a sheepish smile.

"I'm sorry, honey. Bronson is waiting. We can talk tomorrow," she then turned and walked out the door to where Bronson's car was indeed waiting.

WE DIDN'T TALK TOMORROW. She didn't come home the next day. Or the day after, which was Friday, when finally, to make sure she was not completely MIA as she had been several months prior, I called her office. Her assistant assured me she was there, but no, she wasn't available to talk. She was in a "very important meeting." and yes, she'd be sure Diane called me back.

She didn't, and the situation persisted into the weekend. Endless texts and voicemails went unanswered and finally, I went so far as to drive to Bronson's loft and park out front, a discreet distance away. Close enough to see, far enough to not be recognized.

I got there in late afternoon. At midnight I was still there, hungry, and thirsty and completely incontinent. In all the cop shows I had watched as a kid, none ever mentioned needing to piss while on a stakeout. Finally, while I was dreaming of beer and pizza and holding my bladder until it would burst, I saw two dark figures walking down the street. They were holding each other closely and when the light from a nearby streetlamp finally struck them, I could see it was Diane and Bronson. Using the field glasses I took to football games, I could see their faces and more. For one thing, she was not wearing the dress she had worn when running to meet her lover. If anything, the one she was wearing was even more daring than the one I had categorized as "barely there."

Bronson was holding her tight. Was the arm he had around my wife insinuated into the top of the lowcut dress? Was his hand on her breast? Or was my desperate hunger, thirst, and need for a toilet causing me to hallucinate? When she squealed and half-heartedly slapped at his groping hand, I knew there was no hallucination.

They stopped at the front of the building, illuminated by the light at the entryway. He took his hand off her tits and turned her toward him and they kissed. Passionately. Intimately. Not like a bull and a hotwife. Like lovers. Like two people who were becoming one by creating life. I watched as my life cracked to bits before my eyes as they were locked in a never-ending kiss. My heart was breaking as I started the car and put it in gear. So complete was their concentration on each other they paid me no attention. As I pulled from my space out onto the street, I realized something.

I had peed my pants.

## 30

Somehow, I made it home. Once there I got out of my car without cleaning up the puddle on the floor on the driver's side. It would smell like hell, but I was unconcerned. It seemed I had no one to ride in it with me anymore.

It was 1:15 when I made my first drink. Then 1:24 when I made my second and 1:32 when I made my third. Before I made my fourth, I staggered to the kitchen to make myself a sandwich while I still could.

Sometime before 2:30, I fell asleep drinking my fifth drink, leaving my ham and cheese sandwich sitting on the cocktail table half-eaten. Maybe less than half. When I finally awoke at 11:23, the sandwich was on the floor, its disparate parts scattered across the carpet. My drink was still safe in my hand. Priorities. I looked at it and drained the glass.

Before I was physically able to lift myself off the sofa to make another drink, I heard a key in the lock of the front door, after which Diane stepped in. She was wearing shorts, a top, and sandals none of which I recognized. She smiled, which I recognized. I'd seen that same expression right before she kissed Bronson and ripped my heart out of my chest and drove her spike heels through it.

"Hi honey," she greeted me breezily. I showed her. I scowled and didn't say hello back. I was always good at teaching Diane a lesson.

She stood looking at me sitting in a heap. Obviously hungover and deprived of restful sleep. The only thing I had going for me was that the pee stain on the front of my jeans was dried and not readily noticeable. She did, however, sniff the air.

"What stinks in here?" She said, making a face. Looking at her, I shrugged my shoulders and made what for me was a mean face. For other husbands, whose wives had been missing several days with no explanation it probably looked like indigestion. Giving me a confused look, she turned and headed to the bedroom. Struggling, I finally made it off the couch and, moving like a junk car, I followed her, knowing we had to have it out. Finish it. The way I was moving I'd make it to her in about a week.

As it turned out I got there in less than a week, though not a lot less. The shower was going so I guessed she had taken steps to get traces of Bronson off her outer body, even as she was growing a little Bronson in her inner body. I slumped on the bed and placed my face in my hands as the water in the shower kept its steady beat.

I lifted my head when I heard the shower stop. She stepped out of the bathroom still damp and drying herself with a towel. Once she was reasonably dry, she wrapped her wet hair with the towel and placed her hands on her hips. She was naked. Looking at her, I wondered if this was the last chance I'd have to see her naked. She stood there a long time, as though trying to figure out my behavior.

"What the fuck is going on, Jack?" She finally asked.

I stared at her stunned she could be so obtuse. Or maybe stunned that she thought I was so stupid.

"You think I don't know," I said in as restrained a manner as was possible given the circumstance. "But, I know. I fucking know!"

Diane arched her eyebrows in surprise at my outburst.

"Know what?" She asked.

I hid my face in my hands again.

"You know what," my anger was drifting into despondency.

She didn't reply for a long time and by the time I looked up she had thrown on her robe and was storming from the room. If my goal was to finish this, I should have stayed sitting. Started packing. Instead, against my better judgment and all common sense, I followed her. When I got to the living room, I heard glass clinking in the bar area.

She's drinking.

Virtually leaping across the room, I stormed to the bar.

"You can't do that!" I scolded her.

"What? Why?" She asked indignantly. Then she reached into the pocket of her robe and pulled out her phone, looking at the time. "It's 12:30. Don't dare try to tell me we have not started this early. Hell, you were drunk when I got here. Besides, it's a little hair of the dog. Bronson got me pretty toasted last night."

The revelation was startling. In all the time we'd been together, after all the crazy things Diane had done, I had never dreamed she could be so irresponsible.

"You should not be drinking," I declared firmly and as she lifted the glass of scotch to her lips, I snatched it away. When I did, she looked genuinely puzzled. So much so I felt compelled to give voice to my concern.

"Pregnant women should not drink," I said finally.

Never had I seen a look of greater confusion on someone's face.

"What . . . the fuck does THAT mean?" She said in obvious outrage.

When she said that I slammed the glass down so hard it slopped liquor all over the bar. How stupid did she think I was? Maybe the better question was, how stupid had I proven to her I was?

"Diane," I said trying to stay calm, "the games up. I know."

"Know what?" She was screaming by then and had scrunched her face up to look like a clenched fist. So, I thought to myself, she's playing this out. I have to say it.

"I know you're pregnant," I stated flatly, without anger, almost sadly.

Diane's eyes widened and her mouth was agape. She looked like she was trying to speak and had lost the ability. Until finally, she could.

"I'm . . . what?" She seemed genuinely incredulous.

"Diane," I said to her gently, forcing the words out, "I know the condom broke when you were fucking Bronson."

My wife's eyes widened again. Maybe it was the realization I wasn't as stupid as she had assumed. She was speechless.

"I was watching when it happened," I explained. "In case you'd forgotten, you said, 'Oh Shit.'"

Her mouth had fallen open again and her widened eyes blinked. Twice.

"Yes," she responded weakly, having regained her voice. "But that doesn't mean I'm pregnant."

I pulled out one of our barstools and slumped onto it, weak and defeated.

"Honey," I said quietly, with my head down, unable to look at my wife. "I found the test."

There were several minutes of awkward silence, which seemed natural to me at the time. After all, what can you say to the revelation that ends a marriage?

Unless that's not what was revealed.

"Test?" One word, that came from Diane as though it were a question. She seemed genuinely confused. So was I. I didn't know the woman I'd married was such a gifted actress. Obviously, I was going to have to drop it all on her to get a confession. Instead of replying, I hurried to our bathroom, where the small plastic apparatus that was going to cause our divorce awaited me.

"This!" I said holding it out to her once I returned. She took it from me and looked.

"Where did you find that?" She asked.

"In our bathroom. In a vanity drawer," at which point I wondered why I needed to explain. "It's a pregnancy test. A positive pregnancy test."

What Diane did next surprised even me. She didn't yell. She didn't cry. She didn't curse. She put the test on the bar and reached out and took me in her arms and held me, and kissed me tenderly, and I kissed her back. Only after the kiss broke off did she speak again.

"Yes, my darling husband," she said to me tenderly. "It's a positive pregnancy test." Then she held me tighter and lay her head on my chest and I could feel her breath on my neck when she said:

"But, it's not my test."

DIANE EXPLAINED ONCE OUR EMOTIONS QUIETED.

"Women can know without knowing," she explained. "Once she told me I said, 'Dana, you have to be sure.' So, she got this." She held up the test. She didn't want to be alone when she took it, so she came over here and she took it while I watched."

"But, we have known she was pregnant for months," I countered. "Why did you keep it so long?"

"She threw it away after she saw the results," my wife explained. "I dug it out of the trash. I thought she might want it someday. Or our niece might."

"So," I asked, "It's a girl?" Diane nodded.

"I told her she should name the baby Danielle," she said wryly. I laughed and she shook her head.

"I thought it was funny too," she replied. "But, she's actually considering it."

We sat together silently and at peace for a while. Then I explained what I had been going through the past few days.

"So, you were spying on me?" She asked.

"Yup," I confessed proudly. "Just like James Bond."

She laughed and said, "Like Austin Powers you mean." Then I stuck my top teeth out over my bottom lip and said, "Hey baby, wanna shag?" Diane laughed again. Getting Diane to laugh was one of my superpowers.

"Maybe later," she replied. "But first, you need to get out of those smelly clothes. Then jump in the shower and come back and make lunch. I may not be pregnant, but I feel like I can eat for two right now."

The statement brought back memories of the events that caused my initial assumptions.

"There's no possibility?" I danced around, what I meant to be a question. She understood and shook her head.

"None," she stated with absolute certainty.

"But," I continued, unable to let the issue go, "You . . . and me . . . and . . . him . . ."

My wife looked at me with a sly smile and a wink.

"Ever hear of the morning-after pill?" She replied.

# 31

"Why am I taking Dana to the hospital?" I asked Diane nervously. The phone was on the car's speaker system as I drove to my sister-in-law's house.

"Because," Diane said impatiently. "Sean is out of town, as I have explained twice already. I have a meeting with a client that I simply can't put off. I'll meet you at the hospital."

Nodding at the phone I assiduously avoided rear-ending a slow-moving Buick on the assumption that a multi-car pileup would cause Dana to have to give birth in an Uber. Having succeeded in not crashing I was soon pulling into Sean and Dana's drive, leaping out of my car, and ringing her bell. Not quite as quickly, the disheveled and huge mother-to-be waddled to the and threw it open.

"About time!" she snarled. "My bag's in there. Grab it and let's get this fucking thing out of me."

There's an old saying that pregnant women "glow." Dana was not glowing so much as she was radioactive. Since I wanted to avoid an early stress-induced delivery on her front stoop, I picked up her case, helped her get into the car, and headed to the hospital.

"Push Dana push," Diane urged her sister, having taken over coaching duties from me once she arrived from her meeting. I was grateful she had, as I had been piss poor at it when my own children were born. At least then I could crack the joke that "I was there when it counted."

"AAARGH," Dana screamed as she tried to bear down. "I can't. I can't."

"You can," her sister chided her. "And you will. Now push." I had begged to be allowed to sit in the waiting room with Sheila, the reason being, my mother-in-law needed company. My wife then told me not to move. That I "got them into this mess and better not chicken out now." The implication and the threat of violence her tone contained made me pull up a chair and encourage my sister-in-law to push.

"Has somebody called Sean?" I asked, trying to be helpful. The suggestion earned me a scornful look from both sisters.

"We tried," Diane said, "No luck. Maybe you can get a message to him through Armando. They went to Cancun."

"Push, Dana push," I said after, once again having proven my talent at not knowing when to shut up.

Just then, as though to spare me further incriminating myself, the doctor insinuated himself between myself and my sister-in-law. I took that opportunity to sneak out to the waiting room, where Shelia was talking to a certain young man with whom both her daughters were intimately acquainted.

"Hello Jack," he said as he and my mother-in-law stopped chatting.

"Hello Bronson," I replied, never at a loss for a snappy comeback.

Sheila listened intently as I reported the progress of the entry into the world of what would be her first grandchild. Bronson didn't seem as enraptured by the details and in fact, I was wondering why he was there, and in fact, how he knew Dana had gone into labor. Once Sheila went to sit and rest and text relatives what was happening, I found out.

"You were there?" I asked incredulously once we were out of earshot. "When?"

"When she went into labor," he explained.

As had become my custom, I was confused.

"Yes," he said, "That's why she went into labor."

That statement confused me even further until I remembered my first marriage and that sex could induce labor, a fact I tried repeatedly to use to get my then-wife to agree to amorous activity from the time she conceived. It usually didn't work out for me as it did for Bronson, a fact on which I cared not to speculate.

Any speculation on the subject of coital-inspired labor was cut short by a low, angry, and very familiar voice calling my name.

"Jack! JACK!" I turned quickly and saw my wife leaning out the door of the delivery room.

"Get in here," she said commandingly. Then she saw to whom I was speaking, and her tone became much sweeter.

"Oh, hi Bronson," she cooed. "How are you? Thanks for the call by the way." At that point, I knew how Diane knew Dana needed to go to the hospital.

"Think nothing of it," he replied smiling. "Looks like things are working out."

My wife's face brightened, and she smiled broadly and winked.

"Thanks to your kick start," she chirped. Then turning her attention to me again, she growled, "Get your ass back in here mister."

Of course, I did, just as the baby's head was beginning to crown and the delivery was past the point of no return.

Watching the process, I couldn't help but remember the last time I saw Dana's pussy. How it didn't look like that and how I never wanted to see it in either condition ever again.

Finally, after copious periods of grunting and groaning and screaming by Dana, and as much coaching as Diane and I could manage, the baby exited the birth canal.

"Okay," the doctor said to us, "anyone want to cut the cord?"

Diane turned to me and put a hand on my shoulder.

"Honey," she said, "I think this one is up to you."

So, I did, after which the baby was laid in her mother's arms. Dana looked at her daughter with a smile of pure motherly love.

"Welcome to the world, my darling," Dana said to her baby softly. "Welcome, to the world, little Diane."

I watched and I marveled. Out of the chaos that our lives had become, a new life had begun. Now my world would have two Diane's. As peaceful as little Diane looked in Dana's arms, I had no doubt life for me would continue to be a very wild ride.

# EPILOGUE

"Get a move on Jack," Diane chided me. "Tonight, is Dana's first night out and she's texted me three times already."

Meanwhile, as she was urging me to hurry, I stumbled down the hall with an armload of the baby toys she had bought on Amazon. I suppose I could have pointed out to her that I could move more swiftly with physical and not just verbal help. As usual, I did not do that. I merely responded, "Yes, dear."

"You know where the diapers are?" Dana asked me. I replied that I did.

"You remember the milk I expressed is in the fridge?" She asked. I replied I did.

"You know where I keep her extra binkys?" I was holding little Diane and she had a pacifier in her mouth, but I assured her mother I knew where the spares were as my wife dragged her sister out the door.

"Dana, come on," she said impatiently. "Bronson's out front waiting."

Then after giving her baby a kiss on the head and admonishing me to take care of her, she and Diane rushed toward the waiting Mercedes. Bronson was behind the wheel and I was absolutely sure he wouldn't leave without them since I was also sure that was the night he was going to get that long-awaited threesome.

The gentlemanly young man opened the doors for both women, waved to me, and drove off. Then little Diane and I went back into the house and played with a few of the many toys my wife had bought for her namesake and by play, I mean I played with them, and she drooled on them. All in all, we had a fine time, till the doorbell rang. Going to the door, I looked through the peephole.

It was Dan.

After seeing who it was, I went over to the baby who was already starting to doze and picked her up and carried her to the nursery. Placing her in her bed, I went back to answer the door.

"I'm here to see my daughter," Dan pronounced flatly.

"Good evening to you too Sunshine," I replied. My jokes, which could cause my wife to laugh uproariously, had, as usual, no effect on her former Bull. He stood silently waiting, expecting compliance.

"Where's Dana?" Dan asked demandingly. I looked at him and answered without flinching.

"Not here."

He blinked when I said it, and I considered that a win. He flexed slightly under his well, made suit to try and regain the advantage he had always had. That was gone though as I pictured him the way he was the last time he'd been in my house. Naked and cuffed to the cuckold chair.

"Get the baby," he said in response. "I want to see her."

I looked at Dan and didn't reply. He was as always physically imposing. I was alone in the house with the baby, so my options were limited. Sean had moved out weeks before and was living across town with Armando, having decided the mantel of fatherhood which included 3 a.m. feedings, diaper changes, and spit up on his Manolo Blancs weighed too heavily upon him. Then a plan began to form.

Looking at Dan, I nodded, closed the door, and very quietly locked the deadbolt. Once that was done, I got my phone and made a call to someone who was nearby and whom I hoped would help. He picked up on the third ring and after a quick outline of the situation, he assured me he would. Then I went back to the door and Dan.

"She's sleeping," I told him, which was true. "Let's leave her for a bit. She gets cranky as hell if you wake her." This was also true. In that way, she was very like her namesake.

Dan looked at his Rolex impatiently.

"Not too long," he responded. "I don't have all night to hang out."

I nodded and smiled, but behind that smile, I was thinking he had no idea how little time he had left.

Then in the distance came the roar of powerful engines. Several, and they were getting closer. Dan paid it no mind. He considered it mere road noise. To me, it was the cavalry and quickly around the corner, the cavalry arrived.

Seven motorcycles pulled into Dana's drive, the first being ridden by Chet. Dan finally turned and looked as the big man dismounted his Harley as did the other six bikers. Any of the seven dwarfed the would-be bull and as the group got closer, I shut the door and clicking the deadbolt, knew the problem of Dan was now solved.

# ABOUT THE AUTHOR

John Stone is a typical midwestern man with a fascination and a love of powerful women. He has given up his mundane nine-to-five existence to live to dreams and write about them. These are their stories.